T0208527

Fortune Fools

Fortune Fools

Emily Blokzyl

FORTUNE FOOLS

iUniverse books may be ordered through booksellers or by contacting:

iUniverse
1663 Liberty Drive
Bloomington, IN 47403
www.iuniverse.com
1-800-Authors (1-800-288-4677)

ISBN: 978-1-5320-9070-7 (sc)
ISBN: 978-1-5320-9071-4 (e)

Library of Congress Control Number: 2019920137

Print information available on the last page.

iUniverse rev. date: 12/20/2019

With deepest thanks to my Dad, the other member of my favorite book club.-EB

Prologue

Stories of lost treasure involve just about anything you can imagine: from primitive tribes to natural disasters, from mysterious disappearances to hidden passageways in huge castles, from little-travelled locations to any surface on earth. However, many people would agree that some of the most fascinating stories of lost treasure often involve ships, the sea, unfortunate weather and perhaps even pirates. In fact, varied sources seek to convince the world at large that there is still an incalculable fortune buried beneath the world's oceans, though estimates of the approximate value of this treasure ranges so widely that these stories tend to smack of fantasy rather than truth. Regardless, history is filled with tales of large merchant ships, laden with goods and treasure, that were lost at sea. And while a great amount of treasure has been successfully recovered from the ocean floor, there is simply no arguing that a great amount still remains.

In the late 15ᵗʰ century, the once-powerful nation of Spain had been weakened by a long series of expensive and lengthy wars with France, England and the Netherlands. King Ferdinand and Queen Isabella agreed to fund Christopher Columbus' voyages—with ultimately little cost to the crown—in the hopes that these voyages would open the door to new trade routes and therefore new funds for the treasury.

Though Columbus' voyages were not successful in accomplishing their intended goal, they were unquestionably beneficial for Spain. Subsequent voyages to the new world revealed lands that were rich in metal resources and agricultural goods, including silver, gold, gems, spices, cocoa and silk. It wasn't long before Spanish merchant ships began to transport these treasures back to Spain.

By the 1520s, privateers who hoped to weaken their enemy and simultaneously benefit from the Spanish treasure ships' precious cargo made it mandatory for the merchant carracks to protect themselves. To this end, Spain established two convoy fleets, each including galleons that were heavily armed with cannons, in order to protect the merchant carracks from privateers and pirates. Originating from Seville, one convoy fleet sailed the Caribbean and the other sailed the South American ports of Cartagena and Nombre de Dios. The two convoys then rendezvoused in Havana before sailing home to Spain.

In 1622 the Tierra Firme flota prepared for the voyage home to Spain, heavily loaded with silver from Peru and Mexico, gold and emeralds from Colombia and pearls from Venezuela. By this time, the Dutch had joined French privateers in attacking the Spanish merchant carracks, and thus the heavily armed Nuestra Senora de Atocha was placed as the almirante, or rear guard, of the flota.

Built in 1620, the Atocha was rated at five hundred and fifty tons and was one hundred and twelve feet long, with a beam of thirty-four feet and a draft of fourteen feet. She carried the well-recognized square-rigged fore and mainmasts, with a lateen-rigged mizzenmast. She had the high sterncastle, low waist and high forecastle of a typical seventeenth century Spanish galleon and with twenty bronze cannons and eighty-two infantrymen, she was a formidable adversary.

In addition to her duties as almirante, the Atocha was a treasure ship in her own rights. She carried twenty-four tons of silver bullion in 1038 ingots, as well as 180,000 silver coin pesos, 582 copper ingots, 125 gold bars and discs, 30 chests of indigo, 525 bales of tobacco, and 1,200 pounds of worked silverware. It is believed that the Atocha also carried a great deal of smuggled items in order to avoid the quinto real—a twenty percent tax levied by the Spanish Crown against all items shipped from the New World. Whatever the true tally of precious cargo, there is no arguing that the Atocha was one of the most heavily-laden treasure ships of all time.

Along with her treasure and infantry, the Atocha carried forty-eight passengers, consisting of Spanish upper-class noblemen and women, merchants, a surgeon, and an important church official. They too may have hidden their own precious gems, jewelry and valuables so as to avoid paying taxes on these items, further adding to the ship's incomparable treasure.

Under orders of the Marquis of Cardereita, the second half of the Tierra Firme flota, including the Atocha, remained on Havana while the first half sailed off to Spain. Soon thereafter, the Marquis became aware of a Dutch privateer fleet on its way to intercept the Spanish merchant ships, and with the additional threat of seasonal hurricanes, he decided it was time for the rest of the ships to set sail.

On September 4th, 1622, the remaining twenty-eight ships of the Tierra Firme flota raised their anchors and set sail for Spain, setting a course north toward the Florida Keys and the strong Gulf Stream current. As almirante, the Atocha brought up the rear, sitting low in the water with her heavy cargo.

That very night the early northeastern winds of an approaching hurricane began to assault the ships of the flota. By the time the sun rose on September 5th, heavy ocean swells and blinding rain relentlessly battered the ships. Many of the passengers and crew remained below decks for safety, praying and seasick. As the wind shifted to the south, the majority of the flota was pushed past the Dry Tortugas and into the deeper, calmer waters of the Gulf of Mexico. At the rear of the flota, the Atocha, the Santa Margarita, the Nuestra Senora del Rosario, the Nuestra Senora de Consolacion and four other smaller vessels were not so fortunate, and bore the full impact of the rising hurricane.

Violent winds tore sails and rigging to shreds, breaking masts and sending the ships drifting helplessly toward the small key islands and shallow reefs off the southern tip of Florida. The Atocha crew watched in horror as the Nuestra Senora de Consolacion capsized in rough seas. Captain Bernardino de Lugo of the Santa Margarita stood helplessly as his ship was rolled onto the reefs and shattered by the unforgiving waves.

The Atocha dropped anchor in a desperate attempt to remain clear of the reefs, but the inky black waves of an angry sea were no match for the meager Spanish anchor and the Atocha was lifted clear up onto the reefs. The force of the grounding snapped the main mast and breached the hull, and then the waves pushed the ship back into the ocean. Water flooded the ship in seconds, and the Atocha quickly sank fifty-five feet downwards to the ocean floor.

When the storm finally cleared and the sea calmed, all that remained of the almirante was a stump of mizzenmast, barely visible above the surface of the water. The only survivors—three sailors and two slaves—clung to this poor reminder of what had once been a proud and glorious ship. Scattered on the bottom of the ocean, in what was left of the Santa Margarita and the Nuestra Senora de Atocha, were over two million pesos' worth of treasure. It was a treasure that no one was willing to abandon.

In October of 1622, Gaspar de Vargas set sail from Havana, intending to recover the treasures that had been lost to the Tierra Firme flota. He easily found the Atocha, the stump of her mizzenmast still rising up from the water. However, with all the hatches and gun ports securely fastened and the Atocha sitting fifty-five feet below the surface, it was impossible for slaves and pearl divers to hold their breath and remain below the surface long enough to recover all of the guns and treasure from the wreck. As a result, only two small iron swivel cannons were recovered from the main deck.

With the prospect of significant recovery low, Vargas moved west to search for the Santa Margarita, but he was unsuccessful, finding instead the smaller Nuestra Senora del Rosario in the shallows. As he began to salvage her cargo, another hurricane forced him to abandon the ship's graveyard and seek shelter on a nearby island. When the storm passed, Vargas decided to return to Havana for tools that would enable him to successfully salvage the Atocha's treasure. However, when he returned to where the Atocha had last been seen he found nothing; she had been scattered and buried by the second hurricane. Vargas tried desperately to find any trace of the mighty galleon, dragging the sea floor with grappling hooks that came up empty time and time again. Reluctantly, he gave up.

In February of 1623 the Marquis of Cardereita himself joined the salvage efforts and several silver ingots were discovered, but nothing more.

In 1624 Nunez Melian was granted a salvage contract with Spain, and over the next two years he had a six hundred and eighty pound diving bell cast to use in the salvage efforts. In 1626 he returned to the salvage site and, using the diving bell, he was successful in locating the Santa Margarita. It took four years, and frequent interruptions by the weather and Dutch privateers, to recover 380 ingots of silver, 67,000 silver coins and 8 bronze cannons from the Santa Margarita. Despite his best efforts, however, he was unable to locate any trace of the Atocha.

In the subsequent decades, more treasure fleets were lost off the coast of Florida, and Spain continued its efforts to recover its lost treasure until 1817, when the United States purchased Florida and ended Spain's influence in those waters. The Atocha remained hidden, and was eventually dubbed one of the Ghost Galleons of the Spanish Main.

In 1968, a treasure diver named Mel Fisher began a sixteen-year search for the remains of the Nuestra Senora de Atocha. After several years of searching, translations of Spanish documents indicated that the Atocha lay approximately one hundred miles further east than had previously been surmised. With this new information, Fisher's team adjusted their search location and continued their quest.

On June 12, 1971 Fisher's team located a galleon anchor. A few days later, Don Kincaid found an eight-foot-long gold chain, the first piece of gold recovered from the 1622 Ghost Galleons.

In July of 1973, Kane Fisher found a silver bar that matched one listed on the Atocha's manifest.

On July 10, 1975, Dirk Fisher located nine bronze cannons from the Atocha.

In June 1980, Mel Fisher found the ruins of the Santa Margarita and salvaged her remaining treasure, which was valued at roughly twenty million dollars.

Finally, on July 20, 1985, 363 years after she set sail from Havana and disappeared into the ocean off the Florida Keys, the Nuestra Senora de Atocha and her treasure were recovered by Mel Fisher's diving expedition. Approximately four hundred and fifty million dollars' worth of treasure was successfully salvaged from the wreck, finally bringing to an end a mystery and treasure hunt that had lasted nearly four centuries.

At least that's what many believe...But while Fisher certainly recovered a considerable amount of the Atocha treasure, it's quite possible that some remains lost to this day.

Chapter 1

Three minutes. That's how long it took for my life to change. And unlike some individuals whose life path has subtly but definitely shifted, I was not oblivious to the change at the moment it occurred. Even with the imperfect reasoning of an immature mind, I recognized that something was different in my life.

I was two and a half years old.

***

I was born to Martin and Kathryn Durbrin on February 26th, 1979, the youngest of three boys. My name, as written on my birth certificate, is Christopher William Durbrin, but everyone has always called me

CJ. According to my mother, I was going to be named Christopher John Durbrin, a collection of names my mother loved for reasons that remain unknown to me. A week before my birth my paternal great-grandfather, William Durbrin, passed away, and my father thought it only fitting that my middle name be changed to William. My mother agreed and so it was, but the nickname of CJ stuck.

Of the three of us kids, I benefited most from the pairing of genes. I got my father's long legs, blond hair and tenacious determination, as well as my mother's startling blue eyes and fast metabolism. My father told me that I was the spitting image of my mother's Uncle Alexander, but seeing as how I'd never met the guy (he supposedly made a living through connections to the Ukranian mob—something I was certain my father had made up to needle my mother and scare us boys straight) this didn't mean much to me. By the time I reached eighteen years old, I stood six feet two inches tall and I weighed a healthy one hundred eighty pounds.

My brothers and I grew up in Newhall, California. That was back when it was a small, unincorporated town about forty minutes north of Los Angeles, at the southwestern end of the San Gabriel Mountains. It was the sort of place that no one really knew about, and acknowledging it as my home usually elicited an, "Oh, is that near Palmdale and Lancaster?" from Valley residents, who were only twenty minutes away. At that time it was a wonderful place, quiet and sparsely populated. Years later some developer would decide that the area was a real-estate goldmine, and they would destroy just about all of the beautiful natural landscape to make way for cookie-cutter homes and huge shopping outlets in the conglomerate city of Santa Clarita.

The Newhall I grew up in boasted rolling hillsides dotted with majestic oak trees that predated the Gold Rush. It was home to William S Hart Park, a 260-acre ranch named after the actor who had starred on Broadway and in films depicting the Old West.

There was an abundance of hiking and biking trails throughout Newhall and the surrounding towns, and while it was no equal to Yosemite or the Sequoia Forest, Placerita Canyon had a charm all its own. With such an environment, it seemed only natural for us to spend most of our childhood outdoors.

By the time I was two years old I completely idolized my older brothers, toddling after them while they played cowboys and indians, cops and robbers, space rangers and aliens, superheroes and supervillains. Long before I understood the games or the ideas of good and evil, I had established the fact that it didn't matter what we were playing or who my brothers wanted me to be (usually the "bad" guy). I was just happy to be with them and contributing to our games of make-believe. That was, until our first family trip to Disneyland.

If you ask someone what they remember from when they were two and a half years old, the answer you're most likely to receive is, "Not much." Some individuals may be able to dig a bit and bring up spotty memories from around that age–the colors of a favorite dress, the weight and feel of a favorite toy, the strong taste of a new food or the deep, rolling laugh of a beloved family member. For me, the age of two and a half is like a demarcation point—where dark becomes light, obscure becomes lucid and childhood amnesia becomes crystal clear memory.

My memories from before our trip to Disneyland are spotty and vague, just like most childhood memories are. My memories of the day we went to Disneyland, however, and of everything that followed, are as crisp as the memories I've formed in the last 24 hours.

***

On the day we went to Disneyland, the entire family was up by 6 am. This was normal for us. What wasn't normal was the feeling of intense excitement that made the air in the house feel electric. Despite my family's best attempts at indoctrination, I really didn't understand what was in store. I had the vague idea that we were going to visit Mickey Mouse's house, but my brothers were practically frantic with excitement and it was contagious.

Everything that Disneyland works so hard to achieve— an unmatched and entirely magical experience for guests— had its full, intended effect on me and my brothers. I remember being awestruck by the sights, sounds and smells of the park, the rides, the colors, the music and the sheer volume of people around me. I remember walking for an eternity, standing in line until my legs ached and my knees buckled, and riding my dad's shoulders high above the crowd. I remember the relentless heat of the sun, beating down on my head through my hat and prompting a full-body sweat that did little to ease my general physical discomfort. But most of all, I remember the ride.

***

The line for Pirates of the Caribbean began outside in the hot sun, weaving back and forth in front of what looked to me like a spooky old house. When we finally moved indoors into the cave-like atmosphere, we passed multiple signs warning parents that the ride contained dark and scary elements that may frighten younger children. My parents were hardly worried about their brave young boys; even I had done just fine on the Haunted Mansion ride an hour earlier—giggling as all manner of translucent ghosts popped up around me.

My constant complaints about my tired, sore legs eventually worked to my favor and my dad picked me up to ride piggy-back. I remember clinging tight as he carried me through the line, feeling his hard shoulders under his soft shirt. I remember the feeling of his arms, looped under my knees and holding me firmly against his back. I remember the strange, forced semi-darkness, the glow of orange flickering lights and the sound of speakers repeating the endless droning chirping of crickets, the hooting of owls, the creaking of old wood, the croaking of bullfrogs and the calls of night birds. I remember the cavernous ceiling, painted in dark blue with small dots to represent glowing stars. I remember the blue lights and the bright white dots of fireflies. I remember people talking and dishes clinking as we approached the ride boarding area, which ran adjacent to the tables of an indoor restaurant. I remember the mechanical sounds of the ride, the grinding gears as boats were lifted up the ramp to the landing and the metallic click as the lap bars were released. I remember the gentle murmur of voices, some filled with boredom (the hosts and hostesses of the ride), and others filled with excitement (the guests boarding the ride). Most of all, I remember the sound of the water, gently lapping at the sides of the boats as they moved through the river.

Pirates of the Caribbean was hardly the first time I had ever experienced water—after all, we were an adventurous family and spent much of our free time enjoying beaches, lakes, rivers and streams. However, none of my prior experiences with water had produced the visceral reaction I had this time. Despite the water of the ride being anything but the cool, clear, salty water of the ocean, I could feel and taste the sea as clearly as if I were swimming in it with my mouth open. My arms and legs tingled as blood raced through them, and I reached out— as though to grab onto something that only I could sense. My parents told me years later that as we approached the loading dock my breathing came in short, excited puffs—I was sucking air in and holding it for a few seconds before gasping it out again.

After an infinity of waiting, we boarded our boat and drifted into the Louisiana Bayou. From the moment we took our seats in the front row, my brothers were laughing and pointing all around them—at the darting fireflies, the low-hanging moss, a lazy southerner playing the banjo on his front porch, and anything and everything else they could see. For the first time in my young life I didn't mimic their every move. Their antics seemed foolish and childish to me, and I had the feeling that there were far more important things to do. Like remember–I had to remember. My eyes remained focused on the darkness ahead, and my racing heart pounded loudly in my head.

As we approached the dark archway over which a talking skull warned us of what lay ahead, my brothers began shrieking with excitement and anticipation, while my own breathing quickened. My mother glanced down at me, suddenly worried that I might be hyperventilating. To this day she isn't certain whether what she saw on my face was a grin or a grimace, but for the first time she wondered if she had done wrong to bring me on that particular ride.

I was oblivious to my mother's concern, just as I was oblivious to my brothers' mounting excitement. Instead I was riveted, absorbing every sensation, every sound, every sight. The boat moved down a short drop into darkness, and as my brothers screamed in glee I suddenly felt as though I were waking from a long dream. The giddy singing pouring out at us from hidden speakers was distracting, but it still bred a strange familiarity that I reached for and held onto. A second, shorter drop revealed treasure chests, skeletal remains, flickering lightening, growling thunder, howling wind, and torn sails. It awakened a strong sense of urgency–a deep, driving need to find something I had lost.

When the ride came to a close I was confronted by a new, unfamiliar sensation. It was the irritating, nagging feeling that I had forgotten something. I didn't know what it was, but I was certain that if I could just go back, I would remember.

My parents say that's the moment I became pirate-obsessed. I had never been an incredibly fussy or demanding child, but when we got off Pirates of the Carribean I made it quite clear that I wanted to go again. I repeated over and over again a single word: "Member". When my dad asked what I wanted to remember I sighed in exasperation and said, "Evthing!" before stalking off to rejoin the line.

Much to my brothers' dismay, we went back to wait in line for and ride Pirates another four times that day. Each time I tasted that same hint of familiarity, but the memory I was seeking to uncover remained elusive, and I became increasingly irritated. Finally, my brothers and parents tired of making circles, and my mother wasn't certain the ride was doing me any favors, so I was dragged away to another area of the park. None of the subsequent rides, parades or delicious treats succeeded in eliciting anything close to the reaction I had experienced on Pirates. Whenever Mom tried to engage me and asked what I wanted to do, my answer was the same, "Pirates!" But she refused to take me back. She had noticed a change in me, and it made her nervous. She felt that she no longer knew the little boy she had watched grow from infancy. Something was different, and her maternal instinct told her it was neither small, nor temporary.

Chapter 2

My interests changed dramatically after our Disneyland trip. Where once I had been interested in anything and everything, and most especially whatever my brothers were interested in, I now gravitated exclusively toward pirate tales, pirate games and pirate shows, always begging my parents for "More pirates!" Though until then my brothers and I had been inseparable, we were suddenly distant strangers. They tired of playing pirate games after two weeks, and I refused to play anything else. They continued to play on their own together, and I played alone, inventing whatever I needed to fill in for the playmates I lacked.

Despite my obsession with pirates, I was not a bad kid. I went to school, I paid attention to my teachers, I did my work and I didn't get into trouble. Well, at least not any more than other kids my age. There was only one time in my life when I gave my parents any real difficulty, and I have always argued that it was hardly my fault.

When I was about eight years old I moved to a new school and began to have trouble with another kid–a loud, rambunctious boy named Colt who had the rare gift of sweet-talking himself out of just about any problem he found himself in. While it's perfectly normal for any child growing up to have trouble with other children at various points in time, it was the kind of trouble I had with Colt that was memorable. We never argued or fought at all–not with words or fists–but I became terribly upset whenever I was near him. I didn't understand my reaction to Colt, and I didn't try to, but it presented a problem in school where I couldn't even sit in the same classroom with another child without becoming agitated and distracted. Our teachers tried everything they could think of to make us get along–even confining us for an hour to "the friendship circle", a round rug that we weren't allowed to move away from until we had successfully carried on a full conversation with one another–but nothing improved my ability to be near him. Eventually the teachers did the only thing they could, and kept Colt and I separated as much as was possible.

Concurrent to moving to the new school and having trouble with Colt, I began to have nightmares. While I can't remember the content of these dreams (who would want to?), I do remember the gripping fear and anger I felt every time I woke up. In response to my bloodcurdling screams, both my parents would rush into my room and try desperately to calm me down. I would frantically grab for them, sobbing into their shoulders as they gently rocked me back and forth on my bed, rubbing my back and consoling me in soft voices. Following each episode it took hours, and a lot of bright lights, for me to fall exhaustedly back to sleep. After a week of these nightmares my mother took me to a sleep therapist, who recommended a change in my diet. I was restricted from eating wheat products, sugar or dairy, and encouraged to drink a lot more water. I was also dragged outside for a long walk every night, regardless of the weather, and had to spend at least fifteen minutes every day walking barefoot on the grassy field next to our house.

Despite these changes, the nightmares continued, though admittedly with decreasing frequency over time. I learned to control my screams so that while I still awoke in a cold sweat, I no longer alarmed my parents. Eventually, several years after and just as suddenly as they had begun, the dreams stopped altogether. It was a very relieving time for me, because along with the elimination of the nightmares I had just moved to a new school. It was a small private school with a curriculum based around project-based learning, which was perfect for me.

Though I was a fairly introverted individual, I did manage to make and keep a few friends throughout my childhood and adolescence. This was partly due to the fact that I learned, over the years, that while pirates formed an integral part of my own life, few others (actually no one I knew) felt the same way that I did. They experienced the normal, passing fascination, and while they may be interested in touching on the subject for a few moments now and again, they were hardly willing to devote the time and attention to studying them as thoroughly as I did. And so I hid my obsession more and more as I grew older, rarely inviting friends to my house and absolutely never inviting them into my room.

I was picky in choosing my friends, I always had been, and as a result I was never disappointed in my friendships. As a general rule, most of my friends were like me, generally introverted and relatively well-behaved. I guess that's why my parents were so entirely shocked when I befriended Travis—someone who was my polar opposite in behavior, mannerisms and attitude.

Of more significance to me than my unlikely friendship with Travis was the sudden return of my nightmares, a full decade after they had first disrupted my life.

Chapter 3

"CJ?" my mom's voice called through the house. "I thought you had to be there at 3:00. Aren't you ready yet?" Though she was trying hard to control it, her voice was laced with concern.

"Yeah, I'm ready. I'm just grabbing my shoes," I called back from my room.

"Oh, okay. The car keys are on the table. I'm going out to the garden," the back door creaked open. "Good luck!" she said just before pulling the door closed firmly.

"Uh-huh," came my mumbled reply. I finished tying my shoes, grabbed my wallet off my desk, and headed to the kitchen to grab the car keys. They were right where mom had said they were, but what she hadn't said was that they were lying in a pile of multi-colored confetti balloons and miniature "Congratulations!" cut-outs. I sighed, picked up the keys, dusted off clingy confetti pieces, and walked out the front door to the car. It started with a cranky grumble, and I slowly backed it out of the driveway, willing it to keep running. Defiant, the engine coughed and quit, and I sighed as I put it back into park and started it again. The engine grumbled to life once more and I revved it a few times before heading off down the street and to my first day of work.

It was June 1997, just a few months after my 18th birthday. This is a momentous occasion for any teenager—the time when they become a legal adult and gain all the privileges and responsibilities that come with adulthood—but it was especially momentous for the teenagers in my family. It was the birthday when our father informed us that we were no longer entitled to any sort of allowance.

While our mother seemed to do everything in her power to try and stop time altogether, our father seemed to do everything in his power to make sure we grew up, and became independent, as rapidly as possible. By the age of thirteen we were expected to clean our own rooms and bathrooms, do our own laundry, and cook our own meals. Our lists of chores slowly and steadily grew longer, but our meager weekly allowance of $3 never changed. That is, until we turned 18, at which point it simply disappeared.

When we were younger, we could earn whatever extra money we wanted by doing jobs that were above and beyond our weekly chores. However, that privilege had disappeared along with our allowance. My oldest brother,

Glenn, was smart about the whole thing, and obtained a job shortly after his 16th birthday. Our father tried to cut off his allowance at that point, but our mother intervened, pointing out that he was still completing all his chores and was still legally a dependent. My middle brother, Alex, and I were not so eager, and we waited until our 18th birthdays before springing—or rather, crawling—into action.

Our mother tried to sneak Alex and me money whenever she could, but I refused it, knowing how much she went without in order to give everything to us kids. It was only a few bucks here and there anyway, not really anything significant.

Just as Alex had before me, I finally came to the conclusion that the only way I was going to earn real money was by getting a real job. However, summertime was precious time, as it was time away from school obligations. To work meant to give up some of my coveted summertime, but in return I would have some money in my wallet when I did go out. Not to work meant I would have heaps of free time, but hardly the financial means by which to truly enjoy it. After an agonizing internal battle, during which I laid out in the sun in the backyard and nibbled ice-cold watermelon in true summertime fashion, I chose to work.

The next problem to tackle was deciding where to work. I had no delusions of grandeur, but surely I was above working at Wendy's or McDonald's. A few department stores were mass-hiring for the summer and had the draw of indoor air-conditioning, but as a seasonal employee I had absolutely no benefits. I also had to purchase my own uniform, which was hardly appealing to someone who had no money to begin with and would make a rather paltry sum on minimum wage.

I considered working at a local movie theatre, but between the thought of cleaning up stale popcorn and sticky candy in the theatres and running into some of my friends in that ugly uniform, I quickly dismissed the option. Suddenly, every job I thought of seemed demeaning or wrong for me in some way. I began to wonder if I would actually be able to work during the summer after all.

Sometimes you have to step back a few paces to see something that is right in front of your face. It was only when a few of my friends suggested a trip to Six Flags Magic Mountain that I realized it was the perfect place to get a summer job. It was a mere five miles from my house, had excellent benefits (free park entry – need I say more?), provided its own uniforms, and I wouldn't feel embarrassed if my friends saw me there. In fact, I would likely be their hero.

Securing a job at a mass-hiring machine like Six Flags was hardly rocket science. I showed up at the human resources trailer dressed in neat, wrinkle-free clothes, filled out some papers, and smiled throughout the interview. Later I learned that the smiling was key—the park wanted employees who tended to smile freely in casual conversations so that they were more likely to smile at guests. At the close of the interview I was told, a bit unceremoniously, that I was hired and needed to be on-time to training.

Just seven minutes after leaving home, I pulled onto Magic Mountain Parkway and then turned onto the small road that led to the employee parking lot. As I drove past the main guest parking lot, I turned my head to glance at the roller coasters rising high over the park. Their gleaming tracks looked not unlike huge, colorful and twisted spines, turning and weaving over and under themselves in a dizzy game that made passengers shriek with delight and fear.

As I approached the employee parking lot I decided it wasn't worth weaving up and down endless rows of parked cars to find a single empty space, and instead chose a spot in an empty row in the middle of the lot. I shut off the ancient car and opened the door, being greeted simultaneously by a blast of hot, dry air and the sounds of a busy theme park.

"Okay," I said to myself, locking the car and glancing around. The endless clicking and rumbling of roller coasters, the screams of hundreds of excited voices and the repetitive drone of theme music played over thousands of speakers would take some getting used to, but I couldn't honestly imagine a more interesting work environment. I felt the familiar surge of excitement rising within me and I pushed it down. Surely I was too old to feel giddy about working at a theme park. I turned and walked toward the security gate, pulling out my license and training slip to show to the guard.

The guard house was small, with barely enough room for a single stool. The guard sitting inside was leaning back against the wall, his chin tucked down to his chest and his eyes fixed unblinkingly at the parking lot behind me. Though he never looked directly at me, I felt certain he could've described me in detail if asked.

"Hi," I said as I handed the guard my license and training slip. He took them slowly, glancing briefly at my face before looking down at my license. "First day," I tried, and then followed with, "I'm here for orientation." The guard looked back at my face with a raised eyebrow and a look that clearly said, "So?" I felt the tight heat of irritation rising in my chest and throat.

"White trailer to your left," the guard said as he thrust my license and training slip back at me. In seconds he had returned to his stool, leaning back against the wall, chin tucked down to his chest and his eyes fixed unblinkingly in front of him.

"Thanks," I said with barely-concealed annoyance as I took my things and looked over at what appeared to be several dozen white trailers. I walked through the gate and started toward the trailers, more than just a little conscious that I was running short on time and had no idea where I was going.

"Hello!" a friendly voice called out. I turned to see a girl walking towards me, a huge smile on her round face. She was wearing a candy-striped uniform and a visor hat on her head. Despite the uniform's less-than-flattering design, she looked cute and I smiled involuntarily.

"You're here for orientation, aren't you?" she asked as she approached me.

"Yeah. Don't really know where I'm going," I explained. She nodded and giggled.

"Michael didn't help much, huh? He's always in a bad mood when he's out here," she looked over her shoulder at the guard sitting in his little hut. "Not exactly an exciting job," she shrugged. "I'm Beth, by the way," she stuck out her hand.

"CJ," I said, shaking her hand gently. She smiled and nodded, but remained silent, simply looking at me. "So, orientation?" I glanced back toward the group of trailers.

"It's the trailer there, on the far left. The one with the 'C' on the side," Beth pointed. "You'd better hurry–it's just about 3:00. Good luck!" and she walked off.

"Thanks!" I said, watching her for a moment before turning back toward the trailers.

It was exactly 3:00 pm when I stepped into the orientation trailer. I was one of just fifteen new-hires, yet in the cramped space of the small trailer it seemed like quite a crowd. The lack of windows or any other efficient ventilation, along with an assortment of teenage bodies, caused the room to smell like stale, old air mixed with salty body odor and cheap perfume. I suppressed the urge to sneeze and looked around. Lining all four walls were inspirational posters featuring Warner Brothers characters, which I thought was pretty ironic. (After all, a rabbit who hits others on the head with a hammer to serve his personal needs hardly smacks of professionalism.) In the center of the small space was a large horseshoe-shaped table, and in front of the table was a dry-erase board with "Welcome" written on it in large, loopy letters. Around the table were fifteen folding chairs, and on the table in front of each was a large binder decorated with Looney Tunes characters. Several of the new-hires were sitting around the table, flipping through their binders, but most were grouped in a circle in the far corner, chatting and laughing.

Sitting quietly at the table and waiting for the orientation class to begin sounded pretty good to me, and I pulled out a chair and sat down. I glanced around at the others seated at the table and noticed that they were wearing hand-written name tags. A cursory glance around the trailer revealed label stickers and markers on a small desk near the door. I stepped over to the door and quickly filled out a label, scrawling "CJ" in messy letters, and affixed the label over the pocket on my shirt. I returned to my seat at the table and began to flip through the binder. It was standard training material, with the exception of the Looney Toones characters added to nearly every page. *It doesn't matter where I go,* I told myself, *There's no way I will escape some sort of training program. May as well do it with Bugs and Daffy for company.* I continued to scan through the binder, getting a general feel for what was coming. It was pretty straightforward, with company rules and expectations, appropriate employee—excuse me, host and hostess—behavior while "on stage", safety precautions and other basics covered in greater or lesser detail. I glanced up at the clock and noted that it was ten minutes past the hour. It seemed strange that our orientation supervisor was late, especially since punctuality was one of the first company rules covered in the binder. I glanced at the others sitting around the table, but none of them seemed to notice or care about the time. The group in the corner continued to talk and laugh, and I was certain that the lack of a timely orientation supervisor was absolutely the last thing on their minds. Whatever they were talking about, it was far funnier than orientation was likely to be. Being the generally introverted individual I was, I had little interest in finding out exactly what they thought was so funny. Social conversations had rarely been of interest to me, and I had once made such an utter fool of myself in a social situation that I now avoided them like the plague. It was safer at the table, even if it meant coping with boredom. I leaned back in the chair, stretched my legs out in front of me under the table, crossed my arms across my chest, and settled in to wait.

The trainees standing together in the corner suddenly became louder, and one voice rose clearly above the others. My reaction was both instantaneous and unfathomable–I was certain I recognized the voice, and equally as certain that I needed to get away from it. I turned toward the group, looking for the face that matched the voice and failing to find it. My curiosity overrode my reluctance, and I pushed back from the table and stood up, turning toward the group in the corner.

The closer I moved to the group, the clearer it became that a single individual was holding all the attention. It was hardly surprising to discover that this single individual was the owner of the voice I was certain I recognized. I scanned the faces, looking for a familiar one, and was more confused than disappointed when I found none. My attention turned instead to the speaker.

He stood a few inches shorter than me and carried a few more pounds, but there was no arguing that he was decent-looking—as evidenced by the girls staring at him in a giggly daze. He was using obscene gestures and rude jokes to elicit laughs, and while a couple members of his audience seemed personally embarrassed by his antics, the girls were all the more infatuated. He wore two name tags, both of them on his jeans rather than on his shirt. The name tag affixed to the left front pocket of his jeans identified him as "Travis", while the name tag affixed to the right front pocket identified him as "T-Man".

I snorted in ill-suppressed derision, and Travis' head turned towards me. His eyes locked on mine and the fastuous grin faded into what I was certain was a look of recognition. I held his gaze, a cold sweat forming on my back.

Everyone has experienced a brief moment that seems to drag on indefinitely. An introvert could have that moment as he stands before a large crowd, dreading the speech he knows he must give; a nervous mother could have that moment when she spots her child climbing high in a large tree, his foot slipping on a branch; any southern Californian could have that moment each time the earth quakes beneath their feet. Even as I stared at Travis, a bit of defiance mixed in with cold fear, I knew that I would recall these five seconds as though they had been five minutes—or even longer.

"So why did you decide to work here?" one of the girls asked Travis, effectively ending the moment. We both blinked quickly and he turned from me, rolled his eyes and shrugged his shoulders.

"For the free rides – why the hell else?" Travis answered before winking at her. She giggled in response, turning her head coyly to the side. He grinned widely at her before turning back to me, stepping to the edge of the group and shoving his hand forward. I instinctively pushed my own hand forward.

"Hiya. I'm Travis," he said, gripping my reluctantly proffered hand firmly and shaking it.

"CJ," I responded raspily, and then cleared my throat.

"CJ – nice to meet you," Travis said, glancing down at my name tag as though to verify that I had gotten my name right.

"You too," I pulled my hand away and stepped back a little. I had never relished being the center of attention, and I definitely felt uncomfortable with the dozen pairs of eyes trained on me now. Travis, on the other hand, seemed to be enjoying it immensely. He grabbed my shoulder, pulling me further into the group.

"Hey everyone – this is CJ!" he announced loudly, eliciting a chorus of welcomes from the group. I nodded slightly, feeling the heat rise on my cheeks. Travis turned back to me, his eyes once again focused on mine. "We're all trying to figure out who will end up with the worst costumes – care to join us?" I shrugged, and wondered how soon I could escape to my chair at the table. Travis grinned, this time a mischievous one, and thumped me on the back.

"I think the costumes are cute," one of the girls said, flipping hair out of her eyes. Travis leaned close to her, gently brushing against her shoulder.

"Uh no, tight white pants and candy-striped shirts aren't cute," Travis leaned even closer and the girl giggled.

"At least that's better than those stupid pirate costumes," one of the boys chimed in, eliciting agreement from several others. Travis smiled, turning to me.

"What do you think, CJ?" he asked. Not only did he enjoy being the center of attention, he clearly enjoyed putting others on the spot. "Come on," Travis egged me on, "There's gotta be one costume you think is the worst." I shrugged, feeling the heat rise to my ears, conscious of the fact that Travis was the kind of guy who wouldn't let up until I gave him some sort of answer.

"Yosemite Sam," I blurted out. The girls turned towards each other, questions wrinkling their foreheads, and I found myself going on. "Because of those tight pants and huge head and hat – that would be the worst costume to wear during the summer." A couple of the guys nodded in agreement.

"Yeah, any of the characters would suck, just because of the weight and the heat of the costumes," one guy agreed.

"But they get better pay and more breaks than the other positions," another guy argued. I sighed involuntarily as the attention shifted away from me. I slowly stepped back from the group and moved towards the table, aware of the fact that I wasn't invisible and Travis was the kind of guy to notice. *Where is the instructor? They should've been here by now,* I silently pleaded.

"What costume would you want to wear, CJ?" Travis interrupted the others, silencing them and forcing all eyes back to me. I took a deep breath, realizing again that the room was filled with fragrance. Probably the girls, I thought, pouring it on because they thought that's what guys wanted. How wrong they were. That was not to say that we didn't want them to smell nice, but we certainly preferred to keep our senses intact. Three different girls with three different bottles of perfume – I felt the sneeze rising in the back of my nasal cavity, and I fought to suppress it. After a few moments I realized I was successful, only...

"Well damn, you don't have to cry about it!" the guy next to me teased, and the group began to laugh. I used a fist to rub away the tear that leaked out of my eye, smiling and shrugging as non-chalantly as I could.

"Well it's all just so depressing to think about," I said, surprising myself with the quick, albeit stupid, comeback. That wasn't like me at all. I usually thought of comebacks hours—sometimes even days—after the fact. I noticed Travis grinning and nodding at me, and despite my great dislike of open social interaction I grinned and nodded back. Feeling emboldened, I was about to open my mouth and say more (*completely* unlike me – what was going on here?) when the trailer door opened and our instructor stepped into the room.

"Jennifer" it read on her name tag, but she didn't really look like a Jennifer to me. In my mind, Jennifer was tall, thin and blond, with blue eyes, gentle curves and an easy smile. Our training supervisor was of average height, very curvy, and had dark brown hair and hazel eyes. Her small lips curled up into a sweet and slightly crooked smile as she glanced around at us, and I felt the heat rise on my cheeks once again.

As we moved away from the corner of the trailer and took our seats, Jennifer stepped to the front of the room. Travis sat down next to me and leaned in close.

"Hot *damn*," Travis whispered. I shrugged, silently cursing my luck for having him as a neighbor. Travis snickered. "Do you disagree?" he whispered again. I shook my head no, hoping to put an end to the conversation. I watched Jennifer's back as she wrote something on the dry-erase board, the marker squeaking. "Tell me, do you …" Travis' whispered question was cut short when Jennifer turned to face us.

"Welcome to Orientation," Jennifer began, and though no one made a noise, I distinctly heard the sound of a collective sigh rise from the group. Despite the setback of a less-than-enthusiastic audience, Jennifer forged on ahead. "My name is Jennifer, and I have been working here at Six Flags for a little over nine years now. My job today is to help you understand what we expect from our hosts and hostesses, both while 'behind the scenes' and 'on stage.' But before I get into that, let's go around the table and introduce ourselves. Please," she nodded to the individual sitting just to her left. I felt a new wave of panic surge through me and fought the urge to jump up and run from the trailer.

To my surprise, Travis was quiet and respectful as the first five trainees introduced themselves. But as fast as Travis' obnoxious behavior had disappeared, it made a miraculous comeback when it came his turn to introduce himself.

"Hey," Travis began, standing up to garner extra attention, "I'd tell you all my name, but assuming everyone here can read," he pointed at his name tags, "I don't think it's really necessary. I applied for this job because I fucking *love* roller coasters ..." he paused for a moment, glancing at Jennifer and wincing. "Sorry," he added by way of apology before continuing, "I need a job, and seriously – what the hell else is there to do in this desert?" he glanced around the room at all the bobbing heads. Then he glanced back at Jennifer, and as he sat down he added another "Sorry, just totally stoked to be here." She smiled slightly (it was hard to tell if she was offended or not) and gestured at me. As I opened my mouth Travis suddenly hollered, "Hell yeah, CJ!!!" and slapped me on the back. I felt the sharp sting of pain as nerves rushed to the area, and my throat swelled with anger. I wanted to snap at Travis, but all eyes were on me, waiting for my introduction.

"Hi, I'm CJ," I said quickly, before turning to the trainee at my left. The introductions continued around the table, and I took the opportunity to glance back toward Travis. He was still grinning, and when our eyes met he raised his hand, as though to pat me on the back. He obviously thought better of this, nodding his head toward me in what I'm sure was meant to be encouragement. It irritated me, though, as if he were pandering to me in an effort to get a rise out of me.

As the orientation class dragged on, Travis continued to steal the spotlight. He regularly interrupted Jennifer with inappropriate remarks, and while it was doubtful she could be anything but offended, she not only tolerated it, she almost seemed to encourage it. It was a strange thing to watch, her eyes berating him after every comment, but her crooked smile flirtatiously spurring him on. I couldn't understand why she didn't dismiss him from training, and Six Flags employment, as his actions seemed more than just a little insubordinate.

After more than four and a half hours in the small (and incredibly stuffy) space of the training trailer, Jennifer called it quits. We were to return the next day for additional training, but for now we were free, and the park was open for another fifteen minutes. Without hesitation, the entire group wandered into the park and headed towards the nearest coaster, hurrying through the nearly-empty queue toward the ride station. I hung back from the group, excited about walking into the park without a ticket but also reluctant, as always, to participate in a social event—especially with strangers. Travis noticed my hesitation and I knew that my departure from the group would not go without comment. I decided it would be less painful to tag along, and sped up to join the group.

As we moved into the loading rows, filtering down into pairs, I watched Travis move away from the front of the group to come stand next to me. I was sure I was meant to be flattered by his interest in befriending me, but I felt only a vague suspicion. Why me? Was my disinterest in having anything to do with him not as plainly clear as I felt sure it was? We were nothing short of complete opposites, and not the kind that attract or complement one another.

Some little voice in the back of my mind whispered that it was more than our differences that I was suspicious of. Travis was the sort of guy who got into trouble just for the rush of it. He was the sort of guy who found out exactly where the line was and then tapdanced right along it, waiting to see just how much he could get away with. It remained a total mystery to me how Travis had made it through the hiring interview, or what magic he possessed that allowed him to heckle our training supervisor and get away with it. He was rude, obnoxious and self-centered, and the last thing I wanted to do was get drawn into a fake friendship that had me walking over broken glass, waiting for the deep cuts that were sure to come.

As the mechanical gates opened into the station, a twisted knot of anxious excitement tightened in my stomach, either from getting onto the coaster or from being seated with Travis, or perhaps from both. Travis moved forward into the train and I followed, taking the seat next to him and pulling down on my safety harness, latching it between my legs. The ride operators made their way down the train, checking all latches and harnesses, and then signaling the all-clear to the control booth. As the train started to creep out of the station, the thrill of knowing that there was no going back made my heart pound and my blood race.

Just as the train began the first climb, Travis began to holler, elbowing me to do the same. I began with half-hearted shouts, just enough to keep him from heckling me, but as we crested the first climb, I had matched Travis' yells with my own, feeling a genuine excitement and thrill. As we raced down the drop and gravity momentarily failed against the pull of inertia, I suddenly felt that I no longer cared—about anything. I felt freedom and excitement and that nothing else mattered. As we approached the second drop I let out a deep, gutteral and satisfying roar that drowned out Travis' own primal yells. As my roar died I took a deep breath and let out another one, digging deeper and roaring louder.

By the time we re-entered the station my throat was raw. As soon as the safety harnesses were released, Travis turned towards me, placing a hand on my shoulder and looking me straight in the eyes. He didn't say a word, but after a moment his lips curled up in a small smile that froze on his face, revealing something hidden and dark.

It's no secret that people experience fear in different ways. An intense thriller movie can curdle the blood of some and cause hysterical laughter in others. The insects, reptiles or rodents that drive some to scream in terror create warmer feelings in others. Even the furry companions that some feel they cannot live without cause others to tremble in fear.

I myself have some average fears, including a fear of horror movies, snakes, spiders, and sudden, unexplained noises. I also have some irrational fears, ones that I can't identify but that consume me whenever I experience them. What passed between Travis and me that night was far greater than any fear I had yet encountered in my young life, though it lasted a mere second before fading as quickly as the ocean's tide erases footprints in the sand.

Chapter 4

"See you tomorrow, guys," Travis called out as our fellow trainees began to filter down the parking aisles to their cars. Several of them turned back and waved in answer, and a few of the girls giggled.

"This is gonna be an awesome summer," Travis said, looking toward me. "Pretty rad first job, don't you think?" I nodded agreeably.

"Yeah, well. I'd better head home. See you tomorrow," I stuck my hand into my pocket, closing it over my keys as I turned to walk away.

"Hey, uh...can I bum a ride?" Travis called after me. I froze, my hand clasping my keys tightly so they wouldn't jingle in my pocket.

"You don't have a car?" I asked as I turned slowly back toward him. "How'd you get here?" I looked around.

Travis shrugged his shoulders forward in embarrassment. "I don't have a car. Yet. I took the bus. But," he shrugged again, this time more in frustration, "The bus really sucks, you know. It takes you two hours to go 5 miles, because the bus has certain routes and stops every hundred yards and…" his voice drifted off and he shrugged again.

"Yeah, I hear you," I replied. My mind was racing a million miles a second, trying to sort out the problem Travis had just presented me with. I didn't really want to give him a ride–I hardly knew him–but more importantly, I didn't want him to see my old, beat-up station wagon. I found myself wondering whether I could just say I'd come on the bus too, walk with him to the stop and ride home that way (as long as he got off first; I didn't feel too comfortable having him know where I lived either). But then mom's car would be stuck here in the employee parking lot. Maybe I could just stay on the bus until Travis got off and then ride it all the way back to the park and get the car...Travis interrupted my thoughts.

"Hey look, I can see my request has made you uncomfortable. I didn't mean to put you on the spot, and the truth is it would be sorta weird–we don't really know each other. Not really," he said meaningfully. "Don't worry about it, the bus isn't really that bad," Travis shrugged again, and moved as though to walk away.

I suddenly felt torn. On the one hand, he had just given me the perfect way out of my problem. I didn't even have to say anything, not really, and I could just wait awhile before going to the car and driving home. Maybe I could even take the bus to work from now on, or have mom drop me off, in case he ever saw me. On the other hand, I reasoned with myself, while I may not have felt entirely comfortable with Travis, the truth was that he hadn't really done anything wrong. And who knows what kind of life he had—if he didn't have a car who knew what else he did without. Maybe he needed a friend. At the very least, I may be glad I put myself on his "good side" rather than giving him any potential reason to dislike me. I opened my mouth, and heard myself say, "Sure, I can give you a ride!" I even managed to sound cheerful about it.

Travis turned back toward me and smiled what appeared to be a genuinely relieved and grateful smile, "Hey, thanks man. I don't live far, I promise."

I pulled the keys out of my pocket and unlocked the driver's side door, leaning across to unlock the passenger door. Travis pulled the door open and got in.

"Nice wheels," Travis said lightly. I glanced over at him and caught the smirk on his face.

"My mom's," I said by way of explanation. I turned the key in the ignition and started up the ancient engine, grimacing as it began to rumble and moan. "It's old," I explained, and Travis nodded.

"At least you've got a car to use," he said. I glanced over at him again, surprised by his tone of voice. He sounded wistful and sad.

"Yeah," I agreed. I pulled out of the parking spot and drove down the aisle. An awkward silence fell over the car, and just as I was trying to figure out how to break it Travis motioned off to the distance.

"I live in Newhall," he said matter-of-factly.

"Cool," I said, turning onto the small service road that would take me back to Magic Mountain Parkway and the freeway.

"Just off Lyons Avenue," Travis added, looking over at me.

"Great," I said. I was determined not to reveal that I also lived in Newhall, off Lyons Avenue, but I also couldn't help marveling over the fact that we were practically neighbors.

"It's just a little place," Travis continued, looking out at the road, "But it's big enough I could take in a roommate. It would be cool–especially being able to split the rent." He didn't turn to look back at me again, but I felt as though his eyes were boring into my head anyway.

"You live alone?" I couldn't hide the surprise in my voice.

"Yeah. Since the day I turned 18," Travis said matter-of-factly.

"Why?" I asked, immediately regretting it. It wasn't really any of my business, and since he hadn't offered more information, it was rude to ask. But I couldn't help it–as much as I craved all the privileges of adulthood, I could easily admit that I wasn't ready to take on all the responsibilities. The fact that someone else my age was living on their own as an adult intrigued me. Especially since he had just started his first job that day–how could he afford a place of his own?

"Seemed like a good idea," Travis shrugged. "But it's pretty expensive, and even with this new job it'll be tough making ends meet. Figured if I had a roommate, that would be nice. A little company and some help with expenses too, you know?"

"Maybe one of our coworkers?" I offered helpfully. Even if I was ready to move out on my own, I definitely wasn't ready to live with someone I hardly knew.

"Yeah, maybe," Travis said. "Anyone would do really—boy, girl, young, old, I don't care," he drew in a long breath and stuck out his finger, as though to make a point. "I'm just kidding, you know," he laughed. *Okay*, I thought. *Kidding about what? The fact that he lived alone or the fact that he didn't care who his roommate was?* "I still live at home," Travis squeezed out between guffaws.

"So?" I said, before I could stop myself. Travis glanced over at me and stopped laughing.

"Totally sucks, doesn't it?" he asked, and I hid a grimace. I could readily admit that there were things about living at home that bothered me—like enforced bedtimes since I still lived under "my father's roof"—but I got along well enough with my parents and respected them enough that I wouldn't say the situation sucked. "Actually, I probably would move out, but I have a little... problem," Travis lowered his voice and looked out the window next to him.

"What kind of problem?" I asked, curious, but also guarding myself against another rude joke. My mind raced to the first thing I could imagine may have happened—maybe Travis had been arrested for something and was on probation. He probably couldn't move out until his probation period was over. I felt only slightly ashamed that this was where my mind had gone—and quickly—but the truth was that it was Travis who made me feel this way. He just exuded the kind of attitude and energy you expect to find in a defiant teenager. At the same time, since I hadn't seen him do anything dishonest, I silently berated myself for thinking the worst of someone I didn't know.

"It's kind of embarrassing, actually," Travis said, glancing back my way. I was surprised again to see a genuine emotion in his eyes—like he was imploring me not to make fun of him. He turned back to stare ahead into the darkness. "I've got a problem with nightmares." I spun my head to look at him, expecting to see him looking back at me. But he was still looking forward, and seemed not to notice the effect he had created. I turned back to the road, and we drove in silence for several minutes.

"I hate nightmares," Travis finally added, and I glanced over at him again. He seemed genuinely concerned. I nodded.

"Me too."

We drove on in silence, and aside from guiding me to his house, Travis offered nothing more in the way of conversation. As I pulled up in front of a small, dark brick dwelling sitting well back from the street, Travis unlatched his seatbelt and opened the car door. He stepped out and then turned back toward the car, leaning down so he was level with my face.

"Thanks a lot, CJ," he said simply.

"You're welcome," I acknowledged.

Travis nodded and closed the door, walking down his driveway. I nudged the ancient car forward down the street to the cul-de-sac at the end, spun it around and drove on home, arriving to my house just 96 seconds later.

***

That night, for the first time in ten years, I woke myself up screaming in anger. Even as I struggled to catch my bearings and calm myself, I could hear my dad's feet pounding down the hallway. He threw open my door and looked at me, concern written all over his face. My mother's tired, worried face came into view beside him a few seconds later.

"What is it, CJ?" my mother asked, stepping around my dad and making her way over to my bed.

"Nothing, mom, I'm fine. Just a bad dream," I ran my hand over my eyes, but not before catching the look that passed between my parents. There was no mistaking the thought they shared, and it was the same as my own.

The nightmares were back.

Chapter 5

The next morning, as I stood in the shower and let the hot water run over my shoulders and down my body, I thought about the previous 24 hours. My mind kept drifting back to one troublesome fact: after a decade of restful sleep, I had experienced one of the horrifying nightmares that I had previously thought were exclusive to my childhood.

I soaped up my chest and arms, and considered the situation. It was possible it was a fluke—a one-time thing. Maybe I'd eaten something that had disagreed with me, though at the same time I was certain I hadn't eaten anything out of the usual. My mom was worried; I could tell from the way she had greeted me when I got up. Even my dad seemed a little concerned; he had been going out of his way to try to make me smile before he headed off to work. And if I was perfectly honest with myself, I was a bit worried too. Even though I had only just gotten up for the day, I was already dreading lying down and falling asleep that night.

As I rinsed, I considered Travis. Though in retrospect it seemed a little ridiculous that I had been so suspicious of him immediately upon meeting him, there was no arguing that he definitely made me uncomfortable, if only because he craved the spotlight while I did everything to avoid it. He was the sort of guy I would prefer to observe from afar and render opinions on—albeit silently. He also seemed to be the sort of guy who could convince anyone of anything—no matter how absolutely outrageous it may be. The fact that he seemed determined to befriend me made me suspicious of his ulterior motives, though I couldn't imagine what those would possibly be.

I made the shower hotter, letting the water sting my skin for a moment before shutting it off and stepping out onto the rug. Despite the fact that Travis made me feel uncomfortable and I couldn't shake the feeling that the nightmare was somehow connected to him, I still felt like it was better to befriend Travis rather than push him away. The truth is that while the nightmare had made me feel angry and terrified, it had also made me feel that old twinge of familiarity. I wanted to hold onto and explore this familiarity, perhaps in some desperate hope that if I figured it out, I could prevent something bad from happening.

***

There was little chance Travis and I would've developed our friendship if we hadn't been assigned to work rides in the same area of the park, Pirate's Cove. The conclusion of Jennifer's Orientation class consisted of all of us receiving our park assignments. Park supervisors from the locations we were being dispersed to came into the trailer and stood in the center of the room. There were five of them, and they all wore the same navy slacks and light blue shirts. The three men wore ties covered in Looney Tunes characters, and the two women wore matching scarves, tied neatly below their shirt collars around their necks.

Jennifer stepped to the side of the table, yielding center stage to the park supervisors. She indicated to the first supervisor, a stout woman with dull brown hair and said, "This is Margie – she is the food service supervisor for Gotham City. Charles, Tina and Bethany, this is your supervisor." Jennifer indicated to the next supervisor, a lanky young man with short blonde hair and a large smile. "This is James – he is the ride supervisor for Pirates Cove." As Jennifer paused, I realized I was holding my breath. Suddenly it was immensely important to me that I get placed in this location and nowhere else. So important that I considered the idea of quitting should I be placed elsewhere. The very thought was ludicruous–Pirates Cove had little more to do with pirates than butterflies have to do with butter. And yet the idea held–pirates were in my blood and I had to be associated with them however and whenever I could. I glanced up at Jennifer, willing her to say my name. Jennifer looked up at me, as if she could hear my thoughts. "Travis and CJ, this is your supervisor." It took me a moment to realize that the triumphant screaming I heard was in my head. Travis gave a hearty yell and grinned at me, thumping me on the back.

Jennifer finished introducing the remaining supervisors and making location assignments, and then she told us that we would be meeting up with the supervisors again later. First we had to take a trip down to wardrobe to pick up our costumes.

The wardrobe building was a large cement structure that housed the wardrobe room as well as the locker rooms. As we entered the building we were overwhelmed by the smell of cheap laundry detergent and dryer sheets. On the other side of long black Formica counters was a room that looked like five laundromats fused into one. Racks and racks of costumes crowded the floor, while even more mechanical racks paraded even more costumes up and around the ceiling, curving and twisting like a laundry roller coaster. Jennifer asked us to wait in the lobby as she disappeared behind the counter and into the sea of clothes. A few minutes later she returned with the wardrobe supervisor and a stack of papers.

"I need each of you to fill one of these wardrobe slips out. Here is a tape measure, if you are uncertain of size. And boys," she looked pointedly at Travis, "We will not allow you to wear pants that are five sizes too big, show off your underwear and drag along the ground. Before we leave this building, you will all be putting on your costumes for inspection, so you will save us all some time if you choose your sizes correctly." With that, she handed the slips of paper and a box of pens to us.

After jotting down my name, employee number, correct sizes and park assignment location, I passed the form back to Jennifer. The wardrobe supervisor grabbed five slips at a time and disappeared into the racks, bringing back armfuls of brightly-colored clothes that were stiff with starch. I grabbed my uniform and walked back into the men's locker room to put it on.

The costumes were undoubtedly a little cartoonish and not nearly as authentic as my discerning taste would've preferred, but since it was going to be perfectly appropriate for me to scowl and growl "Arrrrgh!" and "Ahoy there, mateys!" anytime I wanted, I decided it was fine. (Though in actuality I wouldn't be caught dead uttering those trite phrases.) As I grabbed up my street clothes, carefully pushing my underwear to the center of the bundle, I turned and checked myself out in the mirror. The costume consisted of black slacks, a red and white striped shirt, and a black handkerchief tied around my neck. There was a second black handkerchief, probably intended to go on my head, but I decided to save that for later, shoving the handkerchief into my pocket. I looked ridiculous, but as I watched my fellow trainees walk out of the locker room for inspection I realized I wasn't the only one. After a final glance in the mirror I turned, and found myself face-to-face with Travis.

"Hey CJ," Travis' face was blank, without his trademark grin, and my insides went stone cold. I opened my mouth to reply, but then decided against it when I realized anything that came out would either be squeaky or shrill. Maybe even both. "Nice to see you," Travis winked at me and turned, walking out of the room.

The chill inside me remained as I chewed over his words. We had been separated for no more than five minutes, and yet he had greeted me as though we hadn't seen each other in a week. And the choice of words–that wasn't his normal greeting at all, and seemed entirely uncharacteristic of him. Nice to see you? What was that supposed to mean?

***

That night, at home in my room, I continued to struggle with what had happened. The cold feeling inside me had remained, and now there was also some breath of familiarity, some hint of déjà vu that dangled wispy threads over my mind but refused to let me grasp them. Finally, I shrugged and sat back on my bed, grabbing the remote and turning to the history channel. There was a special on pirates and I intended to watch it, even though I had seen it once before. As the program neared the end I began to doze off, and with the fresh material my mind easily swirled into nightmare.

Chapter 6

Despite the passing of a full decade, my nightmares had not evolved much from when I was a child. They were of the same variety as the delusional nightmares one has when they are feverish – patchy pictures that make no sense and run into each other over and over until one finally wakes up, feeling as exhausted as if they'd just run a marathon. I had never been able to remember my nightmares once I woke up, but I always awoke with a sense of dread and anger, and I was always drenched in a cold sweat.

Two weeks after I met Travis and the nightmares started up again, I took to drinking five cans of cola just an hour before bed. The subsequent sugar rush and then crash seemed to knock me deeper into sleep and help suppress the nightmares. I still awoke feeling less than rested, but at least I hadn't had an exhausting picture show running in my mind all night long. I didn't tell anyone about the nightmares, because for some reason I felt that if I acknowledged them to someone else, they would become more real. I felt like a kid lying in bed with the covers over my head – if I couldn't see the monsters in the closet then maybe they weren't really there. Deep down I knew I was just fooling myself, and that sooner or later I'd have to face the nightmares honestly if I wanted to get any answers. But I wasn't ready for that. Not yet, anyway.

*****

I often thought that I learned to get along with Travis because he reminded me a little of my brothers. The truth was that he was nothing like my brothers, but he certainly reminded me of someone. There was something about him that caught attention, but it was difficult to pinpoint precisely what it was. I often heard girls talk behind Travis' back about how "hot" he was, but when describing him they never mentioned any of the physical traits that would normally refer to attractiveness. "He's so funny," they'd say, or "He really understood me." You never heard them talking about his hair, his eyes or his physique, nothing but glimpses of a mysterious personality that got their hearts fluttering. Something about him kept you guessing, and you couldn't shake the feeling that he had secrets. Good ones, too, the kind that would get you right past Jerry Springer and straight onto Oprah. And then there was his true gift—the gift of selling any idea to anyone and making them think it had been their idea all along.

Most people enjoy good-natured debates, the kind where their opinions differ widely from the other party. Even if you don't expect the other person to suddenly shift to your point of view, it can be energizing to argue and drive your point home. Of course, there are exceptions—like when the other party attacks not only the point but also the individual who is trying to make it, or like when the other party can artfully twist your words so that you're suddenly supporting their point and attacking your own. That's precisely what Travis could do. And whether it was that skill at work, the twinge of familiarity or some combination of the two, I found myself more inclined to tolerate Travis than I had originally thought was possible.

The initial two-day orientation was just a general indoctrination into park rules and expected employee behavior. Once we got to Pirate's Cove we had a whole training program to complete before we were officially ride operators. After training on the specific rides in our area, which mostly consisted of watching experienced operators at the controls of the rides, we had to pass certification tests. Then we were on our own, which was more than a little alarming when a ride decided to malfunction. My least favorite duty was making the intercom announcements, and not surprisingly this was Travis' favorite duty. Travis found the sound of his amplified voice amusing, and it was hard not to hear him from a few hundred yards away, making his pre-and post-ride safety announcements and heckling the guests during the ride. Supervisors considered it fun and friendly, very much in keeping with the whole atmosphere in the park, but I considered it torture. It was like sitting in a comedy club while the comic pokes fun at you and everyone laughs as you try to figure out how to crawl inside yourself and disappear. "Thank you for your patience. Everyone NOT wearing a ridiculous hat may now come through and find a seat," he'd once said when a troop of young teenagers wearing novelty hats showed up in line.

Despite all this heckling, Travis could be surprisingly friendly and helpful, directing guests around the park and assisting children who had lost their parents. It was the softer side you always hoped to see in someone who sometimes appeared a little rough around the edges. It certainly made me stop and think, since both sides of his personality were convincing, if one of them was real or if they both masked something else. I'm sure it was this curiosity that pressed me to hang on, forging a friendship out of the most unlikely circumstances.

Chapter 7

A year after we met in orientation, Travis and I both found ourselves looking for new places to live. My parents had decided that nineteen years was long enough to support me under their roof, especially since I was now a high school graduate, and they gave me three months to find my own place or start paying a monthly rent, plus utilities. Actually, my Dad decided this. My Mom would've been plenty happy to have me stay for as long as I wanted. She claimed it was because I was her baby and my leaving meant that all of her children really were grown up and on their own. I honestly think she was scared of being alone with my Dad – after twenty-seven years of children and their attendant mess, the house would be deafeningly quiet and remarkably clean and she wouldn't know what to do with herself. Knowing my Dad, I imagined he would probably start running around the house naked and demanding intimacy at odd hours of the day, something else that probably frightened my Mom.

At the same time that my Dad gave me his three month ultimatum, Travis told me that his parents had decided to sell everything and move to Switzerland. I had never actually met Travis' parents (I'd never even been inside his house) but from the occasional tidbits he passed along, this sudden and dramatic shift of lifestyle seemed very uncharacteristic of them. I'd always pictured them as a very quiet and laid-back sort of couple—the kind that would retire and live out their lives in the home they raised a family in. Travis was fairly guarded about their reasons for moving halfway around the world, but he kept alluding to the healthcare system. It was one of the things about Travis that didn't quite make sense, but I didn't press it.

Even in 1995, a few years before the housing market would really begin to soar, the smallest shoebox of an apartment in Los Angeles County was expensive to rent. Since Travis and I managed to get along fine (which really only meant that we didn't openly argue, disagree or fight with one another), we thought living together and sharing living expenses would work. After all, there was no way either of us could afford to live alone and we both figured that any sort of roommate finder service would be a bit like playing Russian Roulette.

Travis said he wouldn't mind moving closer to Los Angeles, perhaps finding a place in La Crescenta or Glendale. It didn't take long to discover that prices were horrible even for a dingy apartment in a neighborhood of ill-repute, much less for a decent apartment in a decent neighborhood. A subsequent search for cheaper housing directed us to some incredible deals – way out in Palmdale and Lancaster. After five weeks of searching through every online rental listing we could find, we finally found a place that would work. It was a small, two-bedroom place in Canyon Country, and while it most definitely wasn't the prettiest thing to look at, it was within our budget and in a familiar area.

It only took three trips, using my parent's long-suffering station wagon, to move all our belongings to the new apartment. While I took all of my pirate paraphernalia from my parent's home, I decided not to remove it from its various packing boxes in the new place. It was therefore no surprise that once we'd fully moved in, the place looked like someone had started to move in and then changed his mind, which was pretty typical of an adolescent bachelor pad. Aside from a stinky old refrigerator and a yellowed microwave, there were no kitchen appliances. The cupboards were empty of anything resembling cookware or dishes, and the pantry was a ghost town that not even the most resourceful mouse could've found a crumb in. The living room was bare of any real furniture, housing an assortment of moving boxes instead, my pirate stuff among them. I had purchased an air mattress to sleep on and Travis had a sleeping bag, which made up the entirety of our bedroom furniture collections. The only thing that indicated someone lived there was Travis' TV. Apparently he had saved up his money until he could buy a Proton WT 3650 – a television with a thirty-four inch screen and a $5,000 price tag. It was no wonder he had never obtained any furniture.

The next five years passed fairly uneventfully. My Mom often called, begging me to come over for dinner every day of the week. As maternal and nurturing as she was, she had never completely warmed to Travis and only occasionally extended the invitation to him as well. Whenever one or both of us made the trip over for dinner, there was always a huge spread waiting. I don't know whether it was because Mom still hadn't figured out how to scale down her cooking to only feed two people or because she had a desperate maternal urge to stuff me whenever she had the chance, but either way the leftovers from her meals covered at least half of our weekly meals back at the apartment. In other words, they were our only real source of decent food.

While I had continued my "career" at Magic Mountain, moving up to a supervising level over the years, Travis had decided to move on to something new after three years at Magic Mountain had yielded him no promotion opportunities of any kind. Though I'm not exactly sure why this was, it did seem that he had spent an awful lot of time in the internal investigations area. Whatever they charged him of they always cleared him of, but the fact that he was suspicious so frequently likely did not sit well with the decision-makers. He also liked to take vacations, lots of them. At least once every two months, Travis was off somewhere for a week or two. It might've been coincidence that as Travis vacationed more frequently his attitude calmed a bit. He wasn't quite as loud and brazen as when I'd first met him. It made me wonder what he was doing on vacation, and I once asked him where he went. He had sat there looking at me for a long moment, like I'd asked him an incredibly complex question that he had to evaluate before answering.

"Just around," he'd shrugged.

"Around where?" I had pressed, really curious now that he seemed to be skirting my question.

"Just around. Camping on a beach, hiking through Sequoia, stuff like that. Just getting away from it all and relaxing for a little," he'd answered. As if to prove his point he invited me on a couple of the trips. I couldn't afford to be off work as frequently as he was, but I went with him to the coast a couple times. It was relaxing, allowing me to unwind and calm down as I was removed from work-related stress and problems. Travis seemed to be as at home near the ocean as I was; it was one of the rare moments where we actually shared a common pleasure.

Travis had acquired a new job even before his last two weeks at Magic Mountain were up. The new job took him out of town quite often; in fact it seemed he spent more time away from home than at it. He said he had found work with a traveling art show that toured the country, renting out mall kiosks for a few weeks at a time. They sold amateur oil paintings that appealed to those who wanted to add some color to their homes on a modest budget. It meant Travis got paid a salary and a commision for convincing people that they needed and wanted the pieces of art he had to sell them—something I had never seen him do but was nonetheless positive he was good at.

I found it kind of odd to have a roommate who rarely ever used his room, but as long as he paid his half of the rent and utilities on time I honestly didn't care. I once had the thought that he must be doing something else and the story about selling art was just a ruse, because he never seemed to give much detail about his travels, even when pressed. I'd ask him about the weather in Phoenix, where he'd been for the Christmas Holiday, and he'd respond that it was "Nice." A couple weeks later I'd ask him about the weather in Wisconsin and get another "Nice." It was just a little hard to believe that anyone, save an Eskimo who was used to sub-zero temperatures, would consider the January weather in Wisconsin to be "Nice".

When Travis was at home, he made a point of staying out of the house as much as possible. He loved going places where he could slide into friendly conversation with strangers, like a bar (he didn't drink) or a dance club (he didn't dance). It was here that Travis divulged some of his secrets—secrets about his difficult childhood. I had been surprised, and a little angry, when I first learned that Travis had spent most of his young life in foster homes and homeless on the street, and that the people who had moved to Switzerland were actually just his last set of foster parents. Then I realized that Travis had never told me differently—he had never actually lied to me about his life or his parents. He had just volunteered so little information that I had assumed the rest. And since I had experienced the comfortable family upbringing I had, it was easy to assume he had as well.

Travis had a special way to truly win someone over, not by moaning and groaning about how awful his life had been and how sad he was, but rather by speaking casually and lightly about it. To hear him talk you would be convinced that he was completely unbothered by his tough past; he often joked openly about it as he went over all the heartbreaking details. He was certain it had made him a strong, charismatic individual, and he was comfortable with that. It was comical to watch someone learn about his past and approach him with sloppy sympathy. Travis would let them carry on for a few moments before shrugging the whole thing off with a story about how he truly considered himself lucky. After all, how many sixteen year-olds made $500 in an hour just by standing on a street corner in scrappy clothes while holding up a cardboard sign? True, the police arrested him under some "city beautification" law and he spent the night in jail, but he'd still walked away the victor with a load of cash in his pocket and a warm meal in his belly.

It would be wrong to say that I ever approved of or encouraged Travis' cavalier attitude about sharing the gritty, and perhaps less-than-honest, details of his life. I considered myself to be pretty honest, and I found it troublesome that it didn't bother Travis in the slightest to play on others' emotions for benefit or take advantage of a mistake.

My Mom had once told me that you could learn a lot about a person by living with them. "Want to know more about someone?" she'd ask. "Live with them for a while and you'll know more than you ever wanted to know." Travis wasn't home a lot, but as time passed I found that I was definitely learning more about him. Like the fact that there was a predictable pattern to his degree of honesty or dishonesty. If he was in a poor mood, you could count on him being relatively dishonest – like defrauding the pizza delivery boy.

"Extra-large with pepperoni and sausage," the kid would say as he unsnapped the delivery bag, "That'll be nineteen sixty-four."

"Extra-large?" Travis would say. "I ordered a medium, what am I gonna do with an extra-large?" The pizza kid would stand, dumbfounded and uncertain of his next move, while Travis would continue. "You know, I call you guys all the time with the same order, and you fuck it up more often than you get it right." Travis used expletives to help drive his point home, and it often worked. The kid had noticeably shrunk back a few inches and lowered his head.

"Sorry sir, I just deliver the pizzas. If you wanna call the shop..." he'd start, leaving enough of a pause that it wasn't hard for Travis to cut him off.

"To what? Be put on hold for fifteen minutes while the pizza gets cold? Damn it," Travis would throw another expletive out as he shook his head in frustration. The kid pulled the pizza out of the box and shoved it at Travis.

"Here, I'll sort it out. What did they tell you for the medium?"

"Thirteen fifty-two," Travis said, pulling the number out of thin air as he shuffled fifteen dollars in his hands. The pizza kid nodded.

"Okay, no problem," he reached for the money, pocketing it and walking off. Travis would turn into the apartment, a smug smile on his face as he took the extra-large pizza that he'd ordered into the kitchen.

Then there were the days when he was in a good mood, and you could count on him to be rather honest and benevolent. I'd once watched him recover some money that had fallen out of someone's pocket. The man had purchased a paper and was distracted as he shoved his money back into his pocket, from where it promptly launched itself and landed on the ground right in front of Travis. It was a nice-sized wad of dough, but Travis barely blinked an eye as he tapped the man on the shoulder and held it out for him to claim.

Despite severe misgivings on occasions when Travis' mood was less than stellar, I wondered if he was really just a good guy who had a rough life and didn't quite know how to adapt. Something in the back of my mind nagged at me, but since six years had failed to bring any clarity to the point, I let it go.

Chapter 8

Travis told me that the house had spoken to him, whatever that meant. He had been wandering down Lyons Avenue one day and there was a big sign hanging in the window of a charity bookstore, advertising a new charity project. It was called Partner Homes, and it was set up to operate very much like Habitat for Humanity, only it was exclusive to the United States. As with Habitat for Humanity, the homes were built by the applicant family and various volunteers and donations. Partner Homes provided a low-cost mortgage plan at a fraction of the interest rate most banks offered. Like Habitat for Humanity, Partner Homes did not seek to simply grant a family a home; they had to work hard for it both by helping with the construction process and by making payments on a reasonable loan. However, to promote themselves and their charitable intentions, Partner Homes was doing something extra special "one time only". They were running a contest called "Help Others, Help Yourself", the winner of which would be the proud owner of a Partner Homes home, free and clear. In the twenty seconds it took him to read the sign, Travis had decided that the home was his.

When I arrived home from work that evening, Travis was sitting at the table, elbow-deep in papers and forms. He looked up at me, excitement clear on his face, and he told me all about it as I removed my light jacket and name tag.

"Well what do you have to do?" I asked casually when Travis was done explaining everything he had learned so far. I grabbed one of the papers and glanced over it. It was something about work ethic. I choked back a "Hah!" as Travis stood up to better gesticulate and expound in his excitement.

"Well the contest is all about helping them build homes. The idea is that the individual or family that helps the most during the month of October wins the contest," spittle flew from his lips and landed on some of the papers. I made a face.

"Where are they building – around here?" I said, taking a step back to avoid being doused.

"No, they're going to put these first homes where they will make the biggest impact – some are in Florida, Louisiana, south Chicago, and someplace else I can't remember…" Travis looked down at the papers, shoving some aside.

"So you're what – going to fly to Chicago for a month and build homes? Do they pay you anything? What about your job?"

"Hell no!" Travis swore without looking up. "I'm no work horse," he added a second later.

"But I thought that was the whole point," I asked, the wrinkles of confusion lining my forehead. "How are you going to win the contest if you don't help them build any houses?"

"The contest is really all about helping the most during a month," Travis explained, clearly having given thought to redefining the contest's intentions in a way I'm not sure the officials at Partner Homes would've appreciated. "I don't have to build any of the homes, I just have to help them get the homes built," Travis shrugged, looking up at me for only a second before returning to paper sorting.

"Well how are you going to help then?" I rolled my hand around as though I was trying to reel the words out of his mouth.

"I've got some ideas…" Travis let the sentence hang unfinished in the air as he rearranged even more papers.

"Some ideas?" I pressed, a cold feeling slowly gripping at me.

"Yeah," Travis answered, offering no more explanation than that. The heap of paper was now slowly taking the shape of two distinct piles. Apparently I had learned all there was to be learned from him at this time, and that was that. My attention shifted to something else.

"Hey, I've been meaning to ask you — have you seen my Best Buy gift card anywhere around here?" I shuffled through some of the papers on the table as I looked for the wayward card. It was a birthday present from my parents — they knew better than to buy electronic gadgets for me since I always took them back to exchange for what I *really* wanted. They'd resigned themselves to the impersonal gift card, which I loved. This one was worth $200 (Mom must have been feeling mighty generous this year), and I'd somehow misplaced it within a week of getting it. I refused to think I'd actually lost it, though that wasn't terribly unlikely for me. Travis glanced up, shaking his head.

"Nope, haven't seen it," he shuffled some more papers around, completing the transformation. "Look, I have some research to do at the library — I'll be back later." I nodded as Travis grabbed his sweatshirt off the back of the chair, shoved his house keys into his pocket, and walked out the front door. I shifted some of the papers in the piles, forgetting my own gift card search as I picked up what appeared to be the legal rundown for the charity contest.

"Blah, blah, blah, must be a legal US resident, blah, blah, blah, making under $25,000 a year… Well shit, that's about half the population," I said aloud to myself. After looking over the rest of the sheet, I set it aside in favor of some television. Something nagged at the back of my mind, but as soon as World's Dumbest Criminals came on, all rational thought left my mind.

Chapter 9

Travis submitted all the required information to Partner Homes about a week later, and then he performed a wonderful sob story for the local media about how rough his life had been and how pitiful it all was. How he got himself on the local media channels I don't know, but I hardly recognized him when I saw the piece – he was wearing a fake mustache and goatee, and had blonde highlights in his otherwise dark brown hair. It was almost as though he didn't want to be recognized, which I didn't understand and was certain I didn't want to.

After the overnight fame generated by his media story, Travis did the real work. He didn't divulge the details of what exactly he did, but whatever it was, it kept him busy and away from home for most of the next six months. He obviously had a careful plan and it must have worked, because on April 5th Travis was announced as the proud owner of a beautiful new Partner Homes residence in sunny Florida.

Despite witnessing all the time Travis put into winning the contest, I never really believed he was going to do it or even *could* do it. It was kinda like when someone's six year-old declares they're going into the backyard to dig a hole to China—you just nod and say, "That's nice," and don't worry about it anymore. But since it appeared that Travis had not only been serious, but had succeeded, I suddenly felt alarmed. I constantly rehearsed my innocence speech as I waited for the inevitable troop of cops to show up at the door, but it never happened.

Now that the hard work and big ceremony were over, the keys were in Travis' hand and a new dilemma presented itself. Getting the house hadn't been his real goal, I now realized. His real goal was to sell the house he had gotten for free. And it wasn't going to work out exactly as he had planned. Or exactly as he had *not* planned, I should say.

Our first real argument happened six years after we had met, and five years after we had started living together. We were sitting in the living room, quietly watching sports highlights and sharing a pizza. Or rather, Travis was watching sports highlights and I was pretending to watch sports highlights. We had long since purchased some cheap furniture for the apartment, and it had become well-worn over the past four and a half years. There were two small chairs in corners of the room, and a round coffee table between them. A large tan couch was the focal point, taking up three quarters of the space and fronted by a long leather ottoman that doubled as an eating surface. The couch was a sort of fabric quicksand, sucking you in when you sat down and refusing to let you get back up without a fight. I was sunk into it now, my knees up around my ears.

"The ceremony was pretty fun, you know," Travis said when the program took a break and the commercials came on.

"Huh," I said, grabbing another slice of pizza from the box.

"They had it set up kind of like a little fair – a petting zoo, food booths, music on a stage, you know, all donations to the charity, that sort of thing."

"Cool," I said half-heartedly.

"They really made a fuss during the presentation too," Travis added, slurping from his can of soda.

"Neat." I had become monosyllabic.

"It's really too bad I can't live in Florida," Travis said around a mouthful of pizza, changing the subject in the hopes that he'd get more out of me.

"Why can't you live in Florida?" I asked, obliging him with a full sentence that showed some interest in the topic.

"That damn heat – it's just unbearable. It's nice to go down for vacation and all, but live there?" Travis scoffed, and stuffed the rest of the slice into his mouth. This left him with a hand covered in grease, which he wiped across his pants leg.

"Well if you can't live down there, what are you going to do with the property you worked so hard to acquire?" I asked, unsuccessful in my attempt to hide the derision in my voice.

"I'm going to sell it," Travis shrugged easily, as if it were the obvious answer and I was the idiot for asking the question. "You know—use the money to buy a house up north. Get the hell out of here – go someplace where you can't *see* the air you're breathing."

"You can't sell it," I pointed out calmly, leaning back on the couch to stretch out my stomach. The couch refused to release my derrière from its grips, and as a result my stretch was disappointing.

"Yeah, I know the market stinks, but I have no carrying costs so I'll just wait as long as it takes to get an offer, no matter how low it is," Travis sipped his coke, and immediately belched. "I'm still making pure profit, since I didn't pay anything to get it," a sly smile. I returned the smile, mocking him.

"No, I mean you really *can't* sell it."

"Whaddaya mean?" Travis asked, taking another sip.

"I mean the small print in the legal contract you just signed, and that you obviously didn't read, says you can't sell the property for a specified time or you automatically forfeit it."

"You mean, for like a month?" Travis asked, turning to look at me. I made a discouraging face. "A year?" Travis asked as a commercial caught his eye. A squirrel was calling banks to get advice on where to store his nuts for the winter. Travis chuckled.

"More like ten years," I muttered. Travis' eyes jerked away from the TV screen and met mine.

"Huh?"

"You can't sell it for at least ten years after acquiring it, or you automatically forfeit it at the time of sale."

"What?!!" The words "no" and "can't" were not in Travis' vocabulary, and when said to him he reacted as if someone had just slapped him hard across the face.

"I <u>knew</u> you weren't paying attention."

"Okay fine, well it kinda messes up my plan, but I can just hold onto it for ten years as an investment property. You know, maybe rent it for a year or two, and then do some upgrades, rent it for another couple years, upgrade again. By the end of the ten years it'll be worth even more than it is now," Travis surmised. "It's not really what I had in mind, and I guess I'll have to postpone some of my other plans, but it could work."

"Oh man," I said lightly, "I almost hate to tell you this…"

"What?" Travis snapped. "Does it say that I can't rent it out either?"

"You really should take the time to read the fine print. After all, that's where all the real terms and conditions are laid out."

"So what?"

"You can't sell the property for ten years…"

"Yeah?" Travis' eyes were staring into mine, searching for the final statement.

"And you have to reside in it for at least seventy-five percent of the time during that period."

"Are you kidding me?!"

"I wish I were," I suppressed a smile. There was something amusing about watching him squirm in anguish at this news. Maybe it was because it felt like justice – after all that he had done that was dishonest, he was getting a little smack in the face that prevented him from getting exactly what he wanted for once.

"What the hell am I going to do in Florida for seven and a half years? What *is* there to do in Florida that is even remotely entertaining?"

"Are you seriously surprised?" I asked, egging him on.

"Hell yeah!"

"You seriously thought that you could just walk into a charity contest, somehow manipulate the system to win the prize, sell the prize, and there would be no problem?"

"What do they care what I do with the prize?" Travis shrugged.

"Dammit, Travis, it's a <u>charity</u>. They don't hand out freebies to people like us for just any old reason," now he had me hot under the collar, something that had rarely happened until I met him, and now happened quite frequently. Fortunately, I was usually able to control my sudden temper flares, but today I felt the urge to let it out.

"Well they should." Spoken like a true five year-old.

"Well they don't. Do you really think you're the first guy to think up ways to manipulate the system? Do you really think they wouldn't wise up and create a tighter deal? For crying out loud…" I reached into the pizza box and took another slice out, biting into it angrily. I wasn't hungry anymore though, and I immediately returned the slice to the box.

Travis remained quiet for another few moments. I could almost hear the wheels turning and the gears grinding.

"So how do they know if you're living at the property for the appropriate amount of time?" Travis asked. I shrugged.

"Why don't you just get the agreement and read through it yourself," I said, wiping my hands on a paper towel to get the grease off them.

"Fine," Travis sighed. "Maybe it's not so bad in Florida. And maybe I can find a loophole before I waste seven and a half years down there," he sat back and picked up the remote, turning up the volume. The message was only too clear—the conversation was over.

Chapter 10

Travis' decision to go down to Florida to handle his new house put me in a tough position. Without a roommate, there was no way I could afford the place myself. Travis and I had been struggling to make the newly increased rent payments over the past year; I could never make them on my own. Or any other rent in Southern California for that matter, thanks to the combination of ridiculous rent rates and inflation. Since I was facing the prospect of homelessness or the horrors of having to take out an ad in "Roommate Finder", and since I truly didn't care about my job, seeing as how it had fallen into a sort of boring routine that never seemed to change, I decided to go with Travis to Florida. I did this while completely disagreeing with how Travis had come by the house, and while still being haunted by the idea that the police would show up at any moment to arrest him. (And probably me too for not doing anything to stop him from doing...whatever it was he had done to get the house.) I knew that I might be in Florida for a month, a year, or the rest of my life, depending on how things went for me there. I didn't care – I was young and had very little responsibility to hold me back from making what others would consider to be rash decisions. The bottom line was that something about Travis haunted me, and I was desperate to discover what it was.

Needless to say, my mother was devastated that her "baby" was moving across the country and would no longer be a mere twenty minutes away by car. My father, on the other hand, seemed greatly relieved. Apparently he had greater expectations for me than to work at Magic Mountain for the rest of my life. However, he realized that my mom was truly having a difficult time and wasn't just being dramatic, and he told her that he had called my Uncle Alexander and asked him to keep an eye on me. My mom seemed both slightly horrified and also slightly relieved to hear this.

In a further effort to soothe my Mom, my Dad offered to buy me a cell phone on the family plan. While half-sobbing that it wasn't the same and it would never be the same, Mom yet accepted the offer and presented me with the cell phone several days later. My Dad had found the least expensive phone their carrier had to offer. It had absolutely no features beyond basic phone service and was almost embarrassing to carry around since it looked ridiculous compared to most of the newer, sleeker models on the market, but it was free and it made my mom happy so I accepted it.

After promising my Mom frequent phone calls and occasional visits whenever possible, I packed up my few belongings and bought a plane ticket, giving notice to the landlord that we were moving out. Our furniture was so ratty and worn down it wasn't worth bringing with us or selling, and we hauled it out to the curb for the garbage truck to cart off. I don't know what Travis did with the TV, but I guess he decided it was too fragile to make the cross-country trip because it was gone when I came home from my last day of work.

Less than two months after Travis won the Partner Homes contest, we arrived in Tampa Bay, Florida. It felt a little surreal, as we rode the shuttle bus across the Courtney Campbell Causeway into Clearwater, to think that this was where we were living now. The whole place just screamed "Spring Break" to me, with plenty of live-music bars and water views in almost every direction. Despite our intended destination north of Clearwater, our discount shuttle ride toured us through downtown Clearwater first, dropping off several passengers as it weaved its way down Cleveland Street and onto Alternate 19. Finally, a good hour after we'd first boarded the shuttle, we were dumped with our luggage at the corner of Alternate 19 and East Tarpon Avenue in Tarpon Springs. As the shuttle drove off in a cloud of noxious exhaust,

Travis and I gripped our luggage and started walking the few blocks to our new home.

The house itself was nothing special, just a small ranch-style home with two bedrooms and one bathroom, located on Athens Street in Tarpon Springs. The materials used in the home were clearly inexpensive – cheap ceramic floors in the kitchen and bathroom, even cheaper Pergo floors throughout the rest of the place. The kitchen was an eyesore with its ugly laminate countertops, faux stainless steel appliances and laminate backsplash. Despite smelling of fresh paint from the walls and new glue from the flooring, the house gave you the distinct impression that it was very old. It came fully furnished, but again, with just the bare minimum in quality. The beds were hard and unwelcoming, the couches small and ugly, and the TVs – well they looked like someone had saved some old sets from the seventies and threw them into the house at the last minute, layering them with a healthy coating of dust and pollen to complete the effect. We learned with disgust that we weren't the first inhabitants; a family of palmetto bugs had found dark crevices aplenty and were happily breeding and scurrying about. Despite all this, the house was free and his, so Travis considered it a palace.

It didn't seem that anything short of demolition could make the place look nicer, but Travis had brought some oil paintings (parting souvenirs from his traveling art show job?) to hang on the walls. They were very Floridian – islands, palm trees and lots of water. In my bedroom he had hung a painting that he knew would make me feel right at home – a pirate schooner on the open ocean. I knew he did it to please me, but he would deny it if I said anything along the lines of showing appreciation, so I just smiled and nodded at him instead.

With a few small touches (candles shaped like pineapples must have been on sale wherever Travis had done his shopping), the house was transformed into a slightly warmer and homely place. I only hoped the palmetto bugs would get the hint and leave us be.

Having lived in California all my life to this point, I was a little shocked to be confronted with the many changes that were part of transitioning into Florida living. The most offensive change in my mind was the complete lack of hills and mountains of any sort – there was just nothing but flat, flat and more flat in every direction. As if that wasn't bad enough, an overpoweringly warm humidity clung to me day in and day out. Air conditioning became my salvation, but even that presented a problem—after all, nothing shocks a body more than moving directly from a warm, wet environment to a cold, dry one. I imagine the warm, moist air must have felt nice for individuals with aching and arthritic joints, but for younger folk like Travis and I, it was extremely unpleasant.

Our new home town of Tarpon Springs was a town of about 25,000 people along the Florida gulf coast. It boasted sponge docks and excellent Greek food; in fact, Tarpon Springs had the highest percentage of Greek-Americans of any US city. The sponge docks, once warehouses for freshly-harvested sponges, had been converted after the red-tide of 1947 wiped out most of the crop. Now they were a rather successful tourist attraction; there was a sponge museum, plenty of souvenir shops, a small aquarium, and of course plenty of delicious Greek eateries. We only lived a few blocks from the sponge docks, and I suspected Greek food would quickly become a big part of my diet.

Four days after we'd arrived I woke up at noon (I don't usually sleep in very late, but I was still on west coast time) to discover that Travis wasn't home and my stomach was growling. We had gone to the grocery store the previous day, making out with little more than some soda, paper towels, a few condiments and a bag of donuts. Not too nutritious, and definitely not appealing to a ravenously hungry stomach. I tugged on a pair of jeans, pulled on a t-shirt, grabbed my wallet and went out in search of food.

Twenty steps down the street I smelled it – a Greek restaurant just around the corner from our street. All thoughts of breakfast burritos and hash browns disappeared from my head as my mouth began watering in response to the delicious aroma. As I approached the restaurant my heart sank. The place was packed, there was no way I'd be sitting down for at least a half hour, and who knows how much longer it would be before I ate. My stomach growled again and I stepped into the restaurant anyway. Maybe a to-go order wouldn't take too long.

I was promised my food in twenty minutes, and ended up waiting for thirty. As a sort of apology for the extended wait time, the waitress grabbed a sticky triangle of baklava and put it in a small pastry bag, smiling at me as she tucked it into my to-go bag. I nodded thankfully and left the restaurant. I wanted to sprint home so I could get at my lunch all the faster, but I managed to suppress the urge down to an impressive speed walk. My key jammed in the lock, and I knew it was just my impatience. I pulled the key back out and slid it in slowly, turning it smoothly in the lock. I strolled directly over to the couch and sat down, throwing my bag onto the coffee table and tearing it open. The souvlaki sandwich was warm and dripping with savory sauce; the first bite was better than I'd hoped it would be.

"What the heck happened to you?" I had looked up from my sandwich just in time to see Travis walk in the front door, soaking wet. He looked like a dog that had been thrown out into the rain, and was sulkily creeping his way back in.

"It's raining," Travis moped as he sloshed across the Pergo floor to the kitchen. The fake wood floor made the puddles look huge.

"Welcome to Florida," I smiled, pushing more of the souvlaki into my mouth and grabbing my drink to wash it down. Travis groaned.

"Tell me it doesn't do this very often," he grabbed a paper towel and mopped his face. His dark brown hair hung flat against his head and neck, dripping onto his shoulders.

"Almost every day during the summer, actually."

"Dear god," Travis said as he threw the wet towel into the garbage and ripped off another. I shrugged and picked up my book off the coffee table. Travis continued to sponge himself dry with paper towels, and then turned his attention to the refrigerator and the few contents therein.

"Huh," he said after a moment, pushing condiments around the shelves.

"Time to go shopping again maybe," I suggested as more condiments were shoved around the shelves. I suddenly realized the position I was in, and quickly stuffed the remainder of my souvlaki into my mouth.

"Ugh," came Travis' empty reply. I heard something slide across a shelf, and he shut the fridge door.

"Where've you been?" I tried to spit out around a mouthful of food.

"Just out for a walk, checking out the area."

"You – walking?" I asked.

"It's been known to happen."

"Hey – how about a trip to the beach this weekend?" I asked, looking up from my book.

"Aren't the beaches here just full of old folk and weird men with metal detectors?" Travis scoffed, popping open his can of Coke. It immediately fizzed, and Travis quickly slurped the rim to prevent it from spilling over.

"Um, no – Clearwater beach is actually a pretty nice beach and the water's good and warm," I said. Travis shrugged.

"What the hell – I don't have anything better to do," Travis said. He pulled a bag of chips from the cupboard and joined me on the couch, flipping on the TV – a Sharp Aquos 65" LCD TV he had somehow acquired (it retailed for $9,000) the day after our arrival, retiring the other, much-aged TV to a nice cozy spot in the garage.

"Okay good – beach trip," I said, realizing I still had a triangle of baklava in my bag. I dug around and found the pastry bag, pulling the sticky pastry out and shoving it into my mouth. Travis glanced over at me.

"What was that?"

"Bakaba," I said around the pastry as it melted in my mouth, crispy and sweet.

"Any for me?"

"Get your own," came my reply as I sucked the remaining honey off my fingers. Travis made a sound, like a grumpy man's "Harrumph", and turned back to the TV.

Chapter 11

Since our status as car owners hadn't changed with the move to Florida (meaning we still didn't own cars,) Travis and I relied on public transportation in order to get places. There were both benefits and drawbacks to this. Among the benefits were riding in comfort while someone else dealt with the traffic, conserving the cash that would have become gas money, and removing the necessity of finding parking spaces in the over-crowded areas you arrived at. Among its drawbacks were waiting on someone else's schedule, stopping every hundred and fifty yards to allow someone on or off, and the two-to-one chance of sitting next to someone who clearly doesn't understand the concept of good personal hygiene.

As Travis and I boarded the bus with our bags of beach gear, it was clear that one of us would fall victim to the hygiene statistic as soon as we sat down. The bus was nearly full and there were no two seats available next to each other. My preferred solution was to stand, but for some reason the bus drivers in Pinellas County became quite upset when you stood while there were still available seats. Travis and I weighed our options as we moved down the rows, playing the odds. I spotted a woman in her forties with a pink bow tied neatly in her hair, and decided she was a good bet. As I slid into the seat next to her, Travis reluctantly slid in next to a gentleman who was easily seventy years old, and clearly not in his right mind as he mumbled cryptic phrases like "And it *would* be, wouldn't it now?" and "Sonny promised me, he promised me real good."

Oddly enough, it turned out that Travis had picked wisely, as I quickly found my nostrils inflamed with the smell of a sour body odor that was poorly disguised with cheap perfume. I turned my head slightly to get a better look at my neighbor, and she obligingly flashed me what would've been a toothy grin if she'd had more than half her teeth. The stench from her breath was worse than the combination of body odor and perfume and I swallowed hard, turning my head away and praying she was getting off at the next stop. As the bus slowed to a stop and she remained comfortably seated next to me, I reconsidered my options. I could suffer through the next twenty miles until the bus arrived at my stop or I could move now. If I moved now there was a chance she would know it was because of her and take offense. Indirectly offending someone was something I hated doing–I was always haunted by what others may be thinking or saying about me. A light breeze from an open window pushed more stale perfume my way and I stood suddenly, moving to a newly-vacated seat three rows back where a quiet young man sat reading his newspaper. As I took a deep breath, I was relieved to discover that my new neighbor was odorless. I could see Travis' back shaking three rows up and I knew he was laughing silently. It was now three to one, my disadvantage, on picking poor public transportation seatmates.

As the bus approached the final stretch of road before our stop it became abundantly clear that we weren't the only ones who had decided to take a beach day. It was only about twenty miles from the house down to Clearwater Beach but it took over an hour and a half to get there. Most of the time was spent on just the last few miles, where we were stuck going a half a mile an hour or slower on the Memorial Causeway. We finally disembarked amid a parking lot of honking cars and began our hike to the beach.

Considering the traffic we had just endured, the beach seemed rather empty. Of course we were used to the crowded beaches of Southern California, where people practically sat on top of each other to be by the water. But then the brand new trend sparked by Hollywood stars probably had something to do with the decrease in beach populations. The fads of tanning excessively and spray tanning had given way to a whole new fad – leaving skin pure and natural. "Pale and beautiful" was the new fashion statement. Celebrities were now photographed showing off their porcelain, pale skin on the red carpet. Just like any fad, there were those that refused to abandon the old for the new. They were impossibly easy to spot on the beach, their rough brown skin looked like over-tanned leather. Almost everyone else carefully hid under light cotton clothing and umbrellas to maintain their natural skin color. Rental companies had set up beach chairs, umbrellas, and shelters along some areas of the beach, and they made a small fortune on those who came to the beach unprepared and then decided the sun was just too bright and hot. And while there were always those few individuals who thought that maybe they could simply sneak into a shelter for awhile, if you sat on a chair or under an umbrella for five minutes someone inevitably materialized to collect payment.

Travis and I chose a spot in between two rental umbrellas, and only twenty-five feet from the water. A woman had set up her beach chair on the sand right at the water's edge, and every time a swell rolled in, the entire bottom of her chair and undercarriage became wet. Even though it looked a bit funny, it seemed like a good idea; it had to be at least ninety-five degrees and with the humidity it felt like a hundred and five. The best idea seemed to be to cool off in the water and then let yourself air dry slowly to remain comfortable. However, I found out with a bit of a shock that the water I expected to feel as cool and refreshing was more tepid, and it only took five minutes to air dry. The solution was to stay in the water, because at least it was hydrating and because it was a heck of a lot cheaper than renting a beach umbrella. It didn't provide full sun protection, but it was better than nothing.

Unlike the boring and empty waters of southern California beaches, these ones were teeming with life and activity. Schools of fish hung around the water's edge, moving whenever someone approached. They looked like they were riding the swells of water, lazily drifting backwards and forwards just feet away from the shoreline. Occasionally a larger fish drifted by, and people gasped or shouted "Oh!". One young teenager claimed he saw some stingrays, and though no one else confirmed it, it was clear that no one doubted him either.

As I trained my eyes on the water further out, hoping to spy a dolphin in the gentle swells, I spotted a fully-clothed man standing in the water up to his shoulders. He was staring down into the water, swaying back and forth as he walked forward slowly, and after a few moments I realized that he had a metal detector in his hands. I couldn't suppress the chuckle that rose in my throat. Using a metal detector on land was comical at best, but searching through chest-deep water with one seemed borderline fanatical. I wondered if he'd ever found anything, or known someone who had found something that was worth the effort. Goodness knows it didn't take much for treasure fever to take hold of you. Men had gone ga-ga over specks of gold that were worth mere pennies, feverishly panning for more even as their life fell apart around them.

"What the heck are you supposed to do in this water?" Travis' irritated question snapped me out of my reverie.

"Huh?" I glanced over to find him standing hunched over and arms dangling as though he were a helpless rag doll.

"Well you can't swim more than fifty feet out apparently," Travis waved his arm at the tall post standing out in the water, designating the end of the "swim area".

"Yeah, I think there's a high sandbar there, perfect for rip tides," I shrugged, borrowing someone else's explanation I'd heard just minutes earlier.

"No waves either," Travis said. "So surfing is definitely out."

"Did you want to surf?" I asked quizzically, raising my eyebrow at him.

"No, but it seems like a waste of beach if you don't have waves," Travis said crankily, shuffling his feet in the water, stirring up sand and sending fish scurrying away.

"I think this is supposed to be one of those luxury beaches where you just enjoy the bathtub water, interact with marine life, sit out on your beach towel, and people watch," I said, closing my eyes and swaying in the water.

"Well that's just boring," Travis answered, splashing the water with his hands. I shrugged, turning back and watching Metal Detector continue to move and sway through the water.

"Go rent a jet-ski then," I suggested, waving lazily down the beach from us where a long row of jet-skis sat out on the sand. Travis opened his mouth to reply but was stopped by a loud "boom!". We both jumped and felt the adrenaline jump-start in our hearts. Our eyes searched the water and we simultaneously spotted the source of the noise. Rounding the edge of the channel was a large pirate ship, moving slowly into the Gulf waters from the waterway behind us. It was ostentatiously painted bright red and flying a large black flag that boasted a skull and cross bones. A large puff of smoke indicated a canon charge (minus the canon ball) had just been set off, and even as we watched, there was another loud "boom!" and another puff of smoke issuing forth from the side of the ship.

"Pirates!" a little boy screamed, either in terror or excitement, as he went running from the water back to the safety of his beach towel and his family. I shook my head, turning to Travis with a grin on my face.

"Wanna go on a pirate cruise?" I asked, only half seriously.

"Avast there ye landlubbers," Travis snarled in his best pirate voice. "We've come to capture your beach blankets and picnic baskets. Aaarrrgh!" I smiled wider, then turned and walked back toward the blankets we'd thrown in a pile onto our "spot".

"Well damn, I've got a seashell stuck in my foot," Travis reached down and picked up his towel, tossing it onto the sand and sitting down. I didn't answer, focusing instead on spreading my towel out flat on the sand. The wind insisted on curling back the corners, and after several minutes of failing to set it straight, I gave up and sat down, leaning back on my elbows to have a look around.

About twenty feet to the north of us a family had decided to make a whole day of it, and had arrived at the beach with what was certainly at least fifty percent of their worldly possessions. There were beach chairs, umbrellas, blankets, towels, sand toys, and several ice chests in their close vicinity. The woman, an overworked mother of two who easily looked ten years older than she was, was trying to find something while being trailed by a sniffling six year-old boy and a whining eight year-old girl. After a few moments the sniffles turned to low wails and the whining to sharp shrieks and the woman turned, her face stern.

"Are you bleeding?" she demanded of her noisy brood. Both children fell silent and shook their heads. "Then stop crying!" she ordered, returning to her search for some item that was either buried among all the rest, or more than likely was the one thing that had been left at home. With premeditated precision that would've made a bank robber jealous, the little girl reached her arm over her brother's shoulder, snatching something from his grasp. She then watched and waited for the obligatory protest, only realizing once it started that she reeked of guilt. She immediately softened her eyes into an innocent "What?" just as her mother turned and glared at them both. The boy sniffed again, loud enough to be heard by his mother but not quite loud enough to elicit another bout of discipline, and plopped down onto the beach blanket. Just a few feet away a young girl, about four years-old, watched the little boy with fascination until her father called her back to their game of catch. Someone shouted loudly from the water, and I noticed a small pod of dolphins just beyond the boundary of the swim area. The man with his metal detector couldn't have been more than ten feet away from the pod, but he was oblivious as he continued to search for his buried treasure. I shook my head, lay down on my back and dug my book out of my bag.

We'd only been at the beach for about an hour and a half when a young girl decided to build a sandcastle next to us. Her fine blond hair was sprinkled with sand, and her pink-polka-dot bathing suit hung loosely around her small, scrawny frame. After carefully packing her bucket tightly she picked it up and shook it, covering me and Travis in fine sand. Her mom rushed in to apologize, but the damage was done and we decided to pick up our towels and head back home.

I always found it interesting that it took getting out of the sun to realize how much damage it had done. As Travis and I rode a mostly-empty bus (thank goodness) back to the house, I realized we were both a little more pink than was comfortable. I pushed a finger against my arm, and watched the white mark slowly fade back to pink. *This is going to suck tomorrow*, I told myself silently. As the bus approached our stop, Travis pushed the call button with a tinkle, alerting the driver, who slowed the bus and opened the door, letting us out onto Alternate 19. We walked silently and slowly up the street to the house, both of us feeling dehydrated and more than just a little sunburned.

As soon as I had opened the front door and we had walked into the house, we collapsed onto the couch (me) and the bed (Travis) for naps.

***

The ship creaked as it rolled on the gentle swells of a calm sea. The sails were shredded and hanging heavy with water, and the ship listed heavily to the starboard side, telling plainly of the sea's fickle nature. The air was thick with moisture, and not the faintest whisper of wind stirred the rigging.

The navigator's feet were planted firmly on the deck and he rolled with the ship, leaning and moving as if they were one. The heavy mist made his clothes hot and heavy, and he was tired. They were all tired. The hurricane had risen suddenly and battered the flota, sending them off course and crippling their vessels, thus delaying their return home to their families. His heart ached at the thought – it had been so long since he had left, and now it would be still longer before he saw his family again, if he ever saw them again.

His duties as navigator had been severely tested by the storm, much more than any storm had done before. They were considerably off course, and a route back out to open seas and the almirante meant braving the very shallows and reefs that had nearly sunk them, and most probably had sunk some of the others. After charting a course under the watchful eye of the Captain, he had been sent away, ordered to join the crew in their lookout for the almirante. Without her they were defenseless against the pirates and privateers who patrolled these waters.

Small white caps along the ocean swells indicated the shallows as they approached them, and the silence on deck became deafening as each man tried to see through the thick fog surrounding them.

"*Where is she?*" *someone asked, their voice sharp with irritation.*

"*We should've seen her by now,*" *another voice affirmed. There were several acquiescing grunts.*

"*She's been crippled by the storm, perhaps even run aground.*" *More grunts. Footsteps approached the navigator and he could feel the visitor's hot breath on his neck.*

"*The Captain is wasting precious time,*" *Alamar's voice was low, barely distinguishable above the creaking of the ship and the lapping of the water against the bow. The navigator turned his eyes to the Captain's quarters, seeing nothing but the glow of candlelight through the door.*

"*He is being cautious, the privateers may not be far off,*" *the navigator whispered, though he hardly believed it himself. "Perhaps he is waiting for others in the flota to join us.*"

"*He is a coward,*" *Alamar sneered quietly. "The almirante was most likely crippled on the reefs. We should go now and claim her for our own.*" *The navigator spun, looking him square in the eyes. Was he really talking piracy? Robbing their own country of its treasure? The navigator's heart skipped a beat as he thought of the dangers, the penalty for mutiny and theft against the crown. Almost as quickly, his heart calmed as he thought of the treasure. His family could be saved from ruin; they would never live in need again. The idea took hold somewhere deep inside and started to grow, powerful greed choking out fear.*

"*The storm spread the flota too far,*" *the navigator replied finally, his voice low. "We have little chance of finding her before another does.*"

"There's always a chance," Alamar's voice was hopeful. "There are many reefs and the weight of the treasure would not allow her to move far."

"It's a big risk," the navigator answered.

"We have worked hard for our country, Duarte, taking many risks in the name of the Crown. It's time we were properly rewarded." Despite a sense of foreboding, Duarte nodded agreement. After all, when <u>were</u> they to receive proper reward for their hard work? The Crown had become greedy, taxing everything it could in order to fund wars that dragged on without resolution and claimed the lives of their brothers.

"What about the others?" Duarte asked. Less people to split the treasure with meant more per share. His mind wandered as he imagined a lovely new dress for his wife and proper meals for his sons.

"Let me worry about the others," Alamar's voice was soft and smooth. How long had he been thinking about this? The fear began to build again, turning Duarte's stomach.

"This is foolish," Duarte said finally, his voice louder than he had intended. He glanced around, but no one had turned. "We don't know if she's foundered on the reefs and lost her crew. Even if we could be certain and knew where she lay, we still may not be able to recover anything."

"She was sitting at the rear of the flota, and far too heavy to move north across the reefs easily. It is more likely that she foundered on the reefs or in the shallows. If she was blown east of us, where should she lie?" the greed in Alamar's voice was thick.

*"Perhaps another half day from us, by dead reckoning,"
Duarte flipped open a compass and consulted his roughly-
drawn map. As he studied it intently, his mind was elsewhere.
Alamar was a strong man and could surely carry through a
mutiny with no ill befalling him. Duarte, on the other hand,
was just a lowly navigator. He folded and then tucked the
smooth leather map back into his pocket, shrugging. "It may
very well be useless as she still could be afloat, heavy with
canons and infantry. If we even find her."*

"We will find her," Alamar said firmly.

*"This is just madness," Duarte said, rubbing at his arm.
The cloth of his shirt was rough, scratching his skin.*

*"Genius is borne of madness," Alamar turned, and
Duarte met his eyes, his breath catching in his throat.
Alamar's lips were curled up in a ghastly smile, and his eyes
glowed red, as if on fire. Duarte felt his blood turn cold.*

I awoke suddenly, my face and neck wet with
cold sweat. It took a moment for me to recognize my
surroundings and realize that I was laying on the couch
in the living room. The house was dark.

"What the heck?" I muttered quietly, the feeling of
déjà vu still strong in my mind. Never before had my
nightmares been so tangible and so clear, as if I were
actually living them. They had always been patchy and
vague, instilling a deep sense of terror without clear reason.
This one had been completely different-I could still smell
the salty sea air and feel the rocking ship beneath my feet.
I blinked my eyes, feeling the sensation slowly slip away,
and rolled onto my side to fall back asleep.

Chapter 12

The next morning I woke up feeling exhausted. I glanced at the clock and frowned, it was 10:00 am. An afternoon nap that rolled into the night meant that I had gone to bed at about 5:00 pm and except for a brief period between 1:00 and 2:00 am where I found myself wide awake, I had slept for seventeen hours straight. No wonder I felt exhausted–I'd had too much sleep. I shuffled into the kitchen and opened the fridge to find breakfast. All that stared back at me was a roll of liverwurst with a hard, exposed edge, and some various condiments. I shuffled back to my room, glancing in through Travis' open door on the way to discover he was already up and gone, and tugged on my jeans, patting my back pockets for my wallet. I pulled it out and glanced inside to find that my cash funds had dwindled to a hundred dollar bill and a few singles. It occurred to me that I had better get off my behind and find a job. Soon.

I hated the idea of spending money on a newspaper when it wasn't absolutely necessary, so I decided to hit up the local library and use their newspapers and resources for free. I knew they would have internet access as well, and I was dying to get on and surf the net for a bit. I trudged down to the bus stop and sat yawning until the bus arrived. I was relieved to discover it was practically empty – there was a woman sitting with her two young children at the back bench and that was it. I grabbed a rail and swung into the first available seat, sliding down into a posture-deteriorating position that would've made any chiropractor shake his head in dismay. The route, like the bus, was nearly deserted, which made the trip down to the library a relatively fast one. I hopped off the bus a few blocks from the library, stopping in a small convenience store for a cup of hot chocolate and a blueberry muffin. By the time I reached the library the only remnants of my breakfast were some crumbs that I brushed off my shirt just before stepping into the building.

I was greeted by two librarians at the front checkout desk who silently looked up at me and nodded almost imperceptibly before returning to their book sorting. They seemed so intrigued by their task that I thought it just as likely that they were surfing the Internet as sorting books. I made my way past the librarians to the computer room, where several people sat before old computers. Technology changed and improved so quickly that libraries simply couldn't afford the newest and the best equipment, and always seemed to be trailing a few years behind. Unfortunately, a few years behind in technology made their equipment appear fairly ancient. I didn't actually mind–it was far more than I owned myself and it definitely worked for my purposes. I found a vacant computer in the corner of the room and signed in, pulling the cheap headphones over my ears and leaning back against the wall as I proceeded to navigate aimlessly through a sea of information – both relatively helpful and completely useless. Of course it was the latter that held my attention the longest as I was sucked into watching videos of bizarre and painful skateboard accidents, stunts gone terribly and painfully wrong, people playing cruel tricks on their "friends", and much more.

After more than an hour of pointless surfing on the net, I decided I had better hunker down and try a job search. I wanted to find something simple – something that I wouldn't have to think about in order to do. I had always thought I would've fit in perfectly on the assembly line at a factory – the simpler the job and less thought involved in my work, the better. Perhaps a jelly bean factory needed someone to ascertain that all beans coming off the lines were perfectly shaped; I could do that. I rationalized that since I couldn't hope for much better than a minimum wage job it was stupid to bother with one that required a lot of skill. I toyed with the idea of getting a job at Busch Gardens (I'm sure my Dad would've just loved hearing about that), but then I quickly abandoned it as too far and complicated a commute using public transportation. As I researched the general Tampa Bay classifieds, an advertisement for Treasure Island caught my attention and I gladly went off on a tangent to learn more.

Treasure Island was a small city about thirty miles south of our house in Tarpon Springs. Original landowners in the area had buried some fake treasure chests, and when they later "discovered" them they eagerly reported the finding of buried treasure to local news groups, sparking keen interest and dubbing the city Treasure Island. Of course, real treasure had never actually been found there, but the idea still grabbed my attention. I clicked on a link to a treasure-hunting sight, and proceeded to get lost in the articles, clicking on new links and being shifted around the web to various sites that claimed to have maps of real treasure sites. It wasn't a steady job with a steady paycheck, but it held the possibility of yielding a fortune and that was interesting enough to keep me captivated. I pictured myself combing the beach with a metal detector and shook my head, fighting back the image I had made fun of only the previous day. There had to be something better, something that was likely to *consistently* yield something of value, even after just a small amount of effort.

I was not alone in my excitement at the thought of uncovering buried treasure. Treasure hunting, and indeed treasure finding, had occurred regularly enough in Florida to gain interest from tourists and new residents every year. Many a Spanish galleon, full of treasure both of historical and cash value, had been lost along the Florida coasts and while some had been recovered, there were still plenty that had yet to be found. Of course it wasn't exactly that simple. Ocean currents shifted, hurricanes stirred up waves and sea beds, and natural sea life grew over everything the ocean contained. Still, if you knew where to look and had the proper tools, there was certainly a chance you could turn up treasure of some sort.

As I continued to browse, I came across a website describing the treasure fleet of 1622, including the Nuestra Senora de Atocha and Santa Margarita. The history of the amazing ghost galleons was long and detailed, and concluded with their recovery by Mel Fisher and his team of salvage experts. As I read through the article I became entirely disconnected from the world around me, and totally immersed in the story of the disaster. I felt as though I could hear the creaking of the ships in port in Havana, waiting patiently as an immense treasure was loaded onto the almirante. I began to mumble, quietly at first, and then more and more loudly. Still, I was unaware of what I was doing until several other library patrons turned toward me and glared, silently demanding silence from me. I stopped to realize that I was arguing with the story, adding details they had missed and correcting minor details they had gotten wrong. Though I didn't particularly remember having done so, I assumed I must have learned about the Atocha and her treasure at least once before in my life—she seemed so familiar to me, and her treasure so entirely real. I read down the manifests that I could find, checking and double checking the items listed there, and silently noting those items that were missing. Even as I read about the spectacular recovery made by Mel Fisher and his team, I wondered if there was still some treasure out there—waiting in its underwater cache to be discovered. In fact, I was certain there had to still be some treasure out there—no matter how detailed and thorough the search had been, there simply was no way to ensure that a team of treasure hunters had successfully recovered every single piece from the ocean floor, right?

Before I knew it, the clock on the wall in front of me showed 4:45 pm and the librarians began to gently but firmly urge people to check out their materials and leave. I had managed to spend the entire day at the library, and yet had failed to accomplish the main task I had gone there for. It was like the housewife who went to the store for a gallon of milk, left with a hundred dollars' worth of groceries, and only realized when she got home that milk wasn't one of them. As I logged off the computer and trudged out of the library to the bus stop, my head was swimming in a sea of treasure. I nearly tripped over a section of cement sidewalk that had been raised by a tree root, and found myself stumbling back to reality.

I must have just missed the bus, because I sat at the stop for nearly a half hour until the next one arrived. Another half hour after that I was walking down our street, still obsessed with the story of the Atocha and toying with the idea of finding buried treasure. However, a car parked a few houses down from ours grabbed my attention, effectively pushing the last cobwebs of treasure-filled thoughts from my mind.

There should have been nothing particularly interesting about a navy Lincoln Town car parked on the street, except that this one had jet-black windows that went way beyond the legal tinting guidelines. This still was not particularly odd, considering that most cars in Florida had darkly tinted windows and quite a few went beyond the legal guidelines. My mind screamed at me that it was a government vehicle, and I suddenly had to fight the urge not to turn around and run quickly in the opposite direction. It was interesting how the presence of government vehicles could make one feel self-conscious, like the driver who finds a police vehicle in the lane beside him and suddenly decides to follow the speed limit really closely. I couldn't help averting my eyes from the car and picking up my pace. It never occurred to me that one of our neighbors may be under some sort of government surveillance, I only knew that I myself was under surveillance as long as I remained in the street. As I stepped into the house, unwittingly sighing in relief, I was immediately confronted by an irritated Travis.

"Where the hell've you been?" he demanded, before turning back to the TV.

"At the library," I responded as I noted the empty grocery bag on the counter. I looked in the fridge and found that a few more items had been placed there. I grabbed a bottle of Dr. Pepper and opened it up. The bubbles felt good, tingling in my throat, but the liquid reminded me that I had hardly eaten all day.

"Since when do you like the library?" Travis shot back, this time not even looking up from the TV.

"Since when do you care?" I answered, shrugging. That was enough to get his attention. He turned my way and frowned.

"I was just wondering," he replied, acting hurt. I didn't fall for it, though I could admit he played the part well. "I mean, what on Earth is there to do at the library all day long?"

"Uh – read," I said slowly, rolling my eyes.

"I thought you wanted to find a job."

"Well yes, looking for a job has been known to involve the reading of classifieds," I rolled my eyes again.

"Did you find anything?" Travis asked.

"I think so, yeah," I lied. I hadn't looked long enough to find anything, but it didn't matter. Besides, I'd decided that finding a job would be a piece of cake, once I actually really looked for one.

"And...?" Travis rolled his hand around on his wrist.

"And what? I'd still have to go fill out an application, do an interview, and get hired," I said testily. "Why are you so concerned about me finding a job anyway?"

"Because we do have some expenses here you know – utilities and stuff. I don't want to starve or anything and I'm not carrying you," Travis shrugged.

"I never said you had to carry me. I don't want to carry you either, so why don't you go get a job?"

"I did," Travis turned back to the TV and flipped the channel. There was a sharp volume difference as the sound blared on and he quickly pressed down on the volume button until the thunderous noise receded to a more normal level.

"You got a job?" I was surprised; Travis never moved that quickly when it came to responsibilities. In fact, the idea that upcoming bills bothered him in the slightest was pretty out of the ordinary. Something else had to be going on, but nothing short of torture would get it out of him.

"Yeah," Travis said, turning the TV volume up a few more notches.

"What kinda job?" I asked, raising my voice above the TV noise.

"Pizza delivery," Travis pulled a bag of cheese puffs to his chest and popped it open.

"With what car?" I asked. We had both obtained our driver's licenses in California the day we had turned sixteen, but neither of us had ever had the means to get a car – not even a real dump of one. Buses had pretty good routes no matter where we lived, and a bus pass was a fraction of the cost of a car and gas. However, a bus was not going to be much help in delivering pizzas unless the customers liked to wait several hours for a cold one.

"The company provides me one," Travis mumbled around a mouthful of cheese puffs that he crammed into his mouth.

"What pizza company provides cars to its drivers?" I felt like a truant officer running through twenty questions.

"It's a small mom and pop shop just down the street. I guess they figured it would be cheaper to purchase a car through the company than have to pay mileage to drivers and worry about their insurance limits. Also gives them a nice little write-off on their taxes. Anyway," he stuffed more cheese puffs into his mouth, crunched them a few times and then shoved them aside into one cheek so he could talk, "I went by the DMV and got my Florida license, so they said I'm good to go."

"Huh," I said, not knowing what else to say. It was definitely possible that he had actually gone out and gotten himself a job. It was also possible that he had gone to the DMV and gotten his license–after all Florida simply requires your old license and a fee for the new one, no tests–but either one of these points of initiative seemed pretty out of character for him, let alone both together in the same day. I stared at the back of Travis' head for another few minutes, wondering what was going on inside. I wondered, as I always did, what his ulterior motives were, and what the possibility was that his actions and motives were responsible for the government vehicle sitting on our street. I opened my mouth to mention the car to Travis and then shut it, realizing that even if he knew exactly why the car was there, he would never admit it to me. After several minutes of receiving no insight, I decided to follow his lead and veg out on the couch, collapsing next to him and reaching for some cheese puffs. It was an incredibly unfulfilling dinner, and I found myself missing my mom for the first time ever.

Chapter 13

Regardless of Travis' *real* reason for doing so, he had indeed obtained a job as a delivery driver for a small pizza shop. Ruth's Pizza was a quaint little shop parked on a corner about five blocks from the house. Their claim to fame was the pizza dough itself – it was seasoned with a secret recipe of rosemary and other spices that really brought out the flavor in the pizza toppings. They sold just fewer than three hundred pizzas a day, up from the one hundred they had sold on average before offering home delivery.

The owners of Ruth's Pizza were William and Ruth Bolzen, a couple who many believed should have been retired for over a decade by now. In actual fact they <u>had</u>

retired nine years earlier, but only for a brief time. For a whole three months they had traveled the country, sight-seeing and visiting with family members in various states. At the end of the three months they had found themselves itching to get home and "back to work". However, after long careers in the employ of others, they were reluctant to rejoin the general rat race. One night, their thirteen year-old granddaughter, Lucy, gave them the perfect solution. They had just sat down to William's homemade pizza when Lucy made a long "Mmmmmmmm," sound. It was William's "basura" pizza – a delicious pesto pizza with kalamata olives, artichoke hearts, sun dried tomatoes, feta cheese, red onions, and a few other tasty tidbits. "This is sooooo good, Papa," Lucy licked her lips as she swallowed the last bite. "You should sell them." William and Ruth locked eyes and smiled; they both knew that it was the perfect solution.

The meager sum in the Bolzen retirement account was certainly not enough for them to permanently retire on, but it was plenty to cover the start-up costs of a small pizza shop. They had never discussed a name for the shop, but William took care of that as a fortieth wedding anniversary surprise for Ruth. They refused to advertise, despite the veiled threats of an early demise from various local advertising sources. They figured word-of-mouth would do the trick, and they were right. There was also sight-advertising, people driving or walking by would see a full restaurant and decide that the food *must* be good, stopping in to see for themselves. It wasn't long before the Bolzen retirement account started to look rather promising, though William and Ruth had no intention of retiring again anytime soon. Occasional vacations to visit family and friends and enjoy various state parks were all they needed, and they loved having something they could always come back to.

Like many other folks their age, William and Ruth were reluctant to embrace change. Ruth's Pizza had no website on the internet, and only a single computer to use for logging and tracking orders and customers. They were constantly approached by family members, friends and customers who felt that they should expand their business further, but they had no interest in investing the extra time and effort necessary to make the business wildly prosperous. Despite their resistance to change, however, William and Ruth finally added home delivery services after being in business for eight years. It wasn't so much a desire to expand the business as it was a desire to continue serving faithful customers and friends who were no longer as mobile as they once were, and who couldn't always make it down to the restaurant for a meal. It was inevitable that the business would grow with the addition of home delivery, but it was worth it to be able to extend the service to the dear friends they had made over the years.

Travis was only the second delivery driver Ruth's had ever had. Patrick, their first driver, had worked for them faithfully for over a year before falling in love with a young lady who had come down to Clearwater for Spring Break. Love will make you do crazy things, and the Florida-born Patrick who had once sworn he'd rather eat palmetto bugs than live in a colder climate, moved to Chicago to get married and start a family. Ruth's had been without a driver for just about a week when Travis walked into the restaurant for lunch and stumbled into a job.

Once Travis had completed reading the employee handbook (which essentially told him to dress nicely and keep his manners in) he was given the keys to his new delivery vehicle. The vehicle that had been bestowed upon him was an old Chevy Cavalier that shook when it went above thirty miles an hour and sounded like it would drop its engine at any moment. Despite this, it was the only car Travis had ever "had" and he loved it. On his second day he tried to convince the restaurant manager to extend their delivery radius, just so he could drive a little further and a little longer. When this request was categorically denied, Travis found that by weaving around the streets, a bit off the direct delivery route, he still got the extra time he wanted behind the wheel. I wondered how long the car would last with Travis driving it, but so far it didn't seem to mind at all. It was probably glad for a bit of excitement in its otherwise humdrum existence.

With Travis once again pulling in a steady paycheck (small though it was), I felt the pressure to get back into the rat race myself. I found a small telecommunications company that promised you could earn $100K a year – emphasis on the "could". Sunriseset sold timeshares to pre-screened clients, those who had shown serious interest in purchasing timeshares over the last five years. That certainly did not mean it was an easy sell, but it did mean that it could be well worth it to stick through an otherwise irritating call in order to make the sale. Base salary was nine dollars an hour, with a confusing bonus system that needed its own fifty-page manual to explain. You were required to make at least five sales a week or you would be terminated, which surprisingly didn't actually do much to raise the morale of the Sunriseset workforce. In fact, the turnover at Sunriseset was so big that it was practically a new company every few days. On the plus side, it was only a ten-minute bus ride from the house and didn't require a resume, lengthy interviews or fancy attire, so I decided to give it a shot.

Sunriseset spent three whole hours training new hires on how to make a proper sales call. There was a pitch and rebuttal sheet to make the sales process relatively idiot-proof. The real trick was getting someone to stay on the phone long enough so that you were able to use the sheet. It was amazing how many prospective customers became suspicious the second a caller asked to speak with them. "Can I speak with Mr. Smith please?" was apparently a horrifying request, and usually elicited the curt response, "Speaking". The next line of "Hello, this is Christopher calling from Sunriseset Properties with an exclusive offer," was often met with angry sentences loaded with expletives, whether they were in an American dictionary or not. "Galdangit! I jus' sat down to enjoy a nice supper and ya'll cretins gotta call me and interrup me with some dagnabit offer while all my fixins get cold! Why doncha just go and..." and so on until I was certain they were blue in the face for lack of breath. There were some hang ups, the rare "No thank you", and even less often there were those individuals who were intrigued and wanted you to continue speaking with them. Ironically, those were the hardest calls to deal with because you actually had to remember all of your lines, sharing the information you'd nearly forgotten just because it was given out so infrequently.

When a trainee first started at Sunriseset he was given a mentor and two weeks' grace period before being turned loose to make the weekly quota. He was expected to work only under the supervision of the mentor, and all the difficulties that were encountered were resolved by the mentor. My mentor was a young woman named Sophie, who was clearly too smart to be a telemarketer and therefore had you wondering what she was doing there. She was tall and slender, with long blonde hair and striking green eyes. She had an effortless, girl-next-door beauty that was genuine and refreshing. Unlike many of the other women in the office, she did not wear an abundance of eye make-up that gummed up her eyelashes or crusted on her eyelids. She wore a light lip gloss that made her full lips look enticing, and her hair smelled of peppermint and strawberries. It took two seconds for me to join the ranks of men who had a crush on her, and only two more for me to notice the ring on her left hand. While it was no surprise (why *would* she still be available?) it was also vaguely disheartening.

I spent an extra half hour in the bathroom the morning of my first official day at Sunriseset, shaving, gluing my hair into place with a thick, gelatinous gel and brushing my teeth. Engaged or not, Sophie was going to be impressed by my general hygiene and appearance.

To make absolutely sure that I would definitely be on time, I took a bus two hours earlier than the one that would've dropped me in front of Sunriseset at 9:00 a.m. As was to be expected I was the first one there, and it was a full two hours later, at 9:30 a.m., before Sophie showed up. By then the office was full and bustling.

"Good morning!" Sophie called as she came running up to the building. "Oh my gosh, I'm so sorry I'm late," she said as she paused to push her hair back over her shoulders. "I just couldn't get any of my appliances to work for me this morning!" she stepped through the door as I held it for her. She walked directly back toward the lunchroom, turning her head over her shoulder to talk. "First my coffee machine timer failed on me, then my blow dryer overheated, and then the toaster oven wouldn't turn on at all. I swear it must be some sort of mutiny or something. Punishment for all the times I short-circuited them," she pulled open a small locker and threw her bag in, closing the door and pulling the key out.

"No problem," I said casually as I wondered what it would feel like to run my fingers through her hair. Not right now, I told myself as I followed Sophie to our work spaces as closely and faithfully as a dog followed its master.

"Alright," Sophie said as we approached the workspace, "Better get started." I pulled my chair out and sat down, grabbing my worksheet and the day's list of names and phone numbers. Sophie sat next to me with her own list, part of my training being exposure to a seasoned pro's sales calls.

As I picked up the phone to dial my first victim...er, customer of the day, I took a deep breath of peppermint and strawberries and sighed, bored already.

***

Sunriseset rented space in a strip mall that was virtually deserted. There were a few restaurants and small shops that inhabited smaller sections of the lot, but a brand new mall a mile down the road had claimed nearly all of the shoppers in the area. It was quite likely that the employees of Sunriseset were the only patrons keeping the small restaurants and shops of the strip mall in business. In fact, one of the employees of Sunriseset had his bachelor party at the small Mexican restaurant just a few spaces over from the office. Strange ritual, really, that a guy would fall in love with a woman, propose marriage to her, and then proceed to get sloppily drunk and become borderline unfaithful on his "last night as a free man". It all seemed pretty weird to me. Then again, I'd never had the guts to get into a serious relationship—I didn't even really date—so how could I presume to know what it was like for those who had fallen in love?

The strip mall itself was set on a lot that was right on the water, and Sunriseset had placed picnic benches out back for employees to enjoy the ocean views while on break. On my first day Sophie stayed inside, helping with one of the other trainees while I took a break. I didn't really care to reach out to anyone else, so instead I focused on the water, watching pelicans swoop down for fish and powerful jet skis go screaming past. As a large, luxury yacht slowly sailed by, my thoughts returned to treasure. It was truly amazing to think about the amount of unclaimed treasure that lay at the bottom of the world's oceans. Despite my best efforts to avoid it, obtaining a metal detector to go hunting for some treasure was starting to sound better and better.

I made it through the rest of the incredibly long and mentally painful day, barely gathering enough energy to smile and nod at Sophie as she got into her car and I began my long walk to the bus stop. When I got home that night the house was dark, Travis was either not home or already in bed. I thought the former the more likely choice – at 11:00 pm it seemed a bit early for him to be sleeping. With the move to Florida he had become somewhat nocturnal, thanks to the time change and a job that never started before 11:00 a.m. It seemed that with our conflicting work schedules I was going to be seeing him much less frequently, just as it had been when he had his traveling art show gig. The thought made me feel lonely, because unlike in California, in Florida I had no family or friends to hang out with. I decided that I could stay up a little later and possibly catch him, so after drinking a cup of water I collapsed on the couch with the remote control. The closing credits for an episode of the Simpsons was the last thing I saw as sleep enveloped me.

***

Duarte stood helplessly on deck, watching as a new type of storm unfolded before him. There was a rock in the pit of his stomach, and he knew it would not be made to go away easily. Despite the authority he had as first mate, Alamar had met with great resistance to the mutiny and had hastily dispatched the Captain and five of the most resistant crew members in a desperate attempt to assert himself. The remaining crew were divided between those that eagerly joined the mutiny and those that only held their tongue so as not to lose their lives. Duarte's sudden promotion from navigator to first mate under the new Captain wasn't sitting well with any of the crew, and he was alarmingly aware of the fragility of his own life. The dissension in the crew made them reluctant allies—not the valuable assets one needed when committing high treason against the mother country. If Alamar was wrong and the almirante was still afloat ... Duarte trembled at the thought of the trials and executions that surely awaited them all.

"Hold her steady to course," Alamar called out to the helmsman. A gentle breeze held in the sails, pushing the ship slowly forward through the shoals. Alamar's eyes were wide, scanning the horizon in search of his prey.

"Captain!" a voice called, and Alamar turned toward the sound. The young ship's boy was standing at the port rail, his arm extended out toward the water. "A mizzenmast, in the water," he continued.

"Where is she?" Alamar asked greedily, his eyes on the water.

"*There,*" *Duarte pointed into the water. The stub of a broken mizzenmast stared out from the gentle swells, like a raised arm pleading for rescue.*

"*Bring her about!*" *Alamar called, and then a moment later,* "*Let go the anchor!*" *Duarte stood at the rail, staring down into the ocean depths. It was hard to tell what lay beneath, whether it was truly the hull of the almirante or just racing shadows.*

"*Is it her?*" *Alamar asked quietly. His voice carried with it a chilling coldness, and Duarte drew back from him and shivered involuntarily.*

"*I can't tell,*" *Duarte answered.*

"*We'll send two divers down,*" *Alamar suggested.* "*They can ascertain her position.*"

"*What about the crew?*" *Duarte asked nervously.*

"*Never mind the crew,*" *Alamar's voice was cold.* "*They will do as they are told. Once we have the treasure, it won't matter anyway.*" *Something about the way he said this did not inspire trust, and for the first time Duarte questioned how far Alamar was willing to go in his greed.*

"*There will be more ships,*" *Duarte said quietly, scanning the horizon.* "*Surely they will send a fleet of ships to recover her.*"

"*Use the slaves,*" *Alamar said, ignoring Duarte's concerns. He well knew that they would not be alone out here for long, and their chance of recovering all or even most of the bounty was next to nothing. But it wouldn't take all the bounty, or even half of it, for them to live well. Greed once again turned Duarte's heart cold, and he felt as resolute as ever.*

Alamar turned and Duarte felt his heart quicken, rising into his throat.

"Do it," Alamar said, turning away.

I sat up suddenly, shaken from my dream by the sensation of wetness. My entire body was soaked with sweat, and I couldn't help the thought that maybe I'd had an accident. My skin felt cool and clammy, and I rubbed my arm across my forehead, feeling for the fever I was certain had to be there. My head was cool, my hand coming back wet with perspiration. I stood, hardly noticing the wet stain I'd left on the couch, and walked into the bathroom. I turned on the light and pulled on the faucet, sloshing cool water over my face and neck before using a towel to pat it dry. As I glanced up into the mirror I stifled a yell of surprise, startled by the strange face staring back at me. Long, dark hair, dark eyes and a beard covered a face that was at least forty years old. Even as I stared at the strange face I felt the warmth of familiarity staring back at me. Something ... so familiar ... and still so strange. I blinked, and it was gone, my own face looking back at me in the mirror. I stood there for what must have been an eternity, trying to ascertain whether what had just happened was real, or simply the residue of yet another nightmare. Finally, the sensation of familiarity slipped away and I decided it hadn't been real at all.

Flipping the light off, I stepped into the hallway, pausing for a moment to listen. Above the loud beating of my own heart, I could hear the gentle snoring that indicated Travis was home and in bed. I walked into my bedroom, threw my covers back, stripped off my wet clothes and sank into bed and restless sleep.

Chapter 14

"Hi Mom," I said as soon as she answered. I heard a gasp, and then a suppressed squeal.

"Oh honey! It's so nice to hear from you! Martin – CJ's on the phone!" she called to my Dad, without moving the phone from her mouth. My ear rang in discomfort. "I was just talking with Dad about you, wondering how you were doing. You know I left a message for you three days ago and then again yesterday…" Oh great, a long distance guilt trip–who knew it was possible.

"I know, Mom, I've been busy," I excused myself.

"Too busy to call your mom for five minutes?" she asked, pressing harder.

"No Mom, not too busy for you. Just...busy..." I trailed off, failing to find a replacement excuse.

"Are you feeling okay honey?" And just like that, she moved from guilt trip to nursemaid. Actually, it was what I wanted to hear. Somehow it seemed easier to let her ask and then confess slowly, as if it was really not a big deal.

"I'm okay, just tired. I'm having a little trouble sleeping."

"What kind of trouble? You know your father has restless legs, it keeps me up more than him, but I've heard recently from Betty, you know that friend of mine who went to nursing school and then decided to go off and be an aesthetician, well she said..." my Mom carried on as I shook my head, holding the phone away from my ear and pressing my free hand to my forehead. "Anyway, that's not important, but what is important is that Betty told me restless legs may very well be genetic. The good news is that if you catch it early enough, you just may be able to take something to stop it. Some kind of weird-sounding herb, I think. Farnel-something maybe? Martin, dear, do you remember that herb Betty told us would help your restless legs?" a pause, punctuated by a faint grumble from my Dad. "Oh you're no help at all. Honestly CJ, I don't know what's gotten into him these days. Hardly looks up from his newspaper anymore, as if I'm not even here." Another grumble from my Dad somewhere in the background.

"No, it's not restless legs, just some weird recurring dreams and night sweats. I don't think it's anything to worry about," I said. All I needed was a confirmation phrase from her – "Oh sweetheart, that just sounds like too much sun. Drink more water, you'll be fine," something like that. I paused, waiting for it, hoping for it, even though deep down inside I knew it wouldn't come. Not this time. It seemed like an infinity of time passed before my mom answered.

"Well dear, that sounds like those episodes you kept having when you were younger. Remember those? You would wake up screaming about something…it was the same thing, over and over again. Oh what was it?" she trailed off, thinking and perhaps even forgetting that I was on the other end of the line. I cleared my throat, and heard her suck in her breath. "Well if it's really bothering you, there's no harm in going to see a doctor. There are those naturopathic doctors all over the place now, I'm sure you'd be able to find one down there."

"I dunno," I said uncertainly. It wasn't that I had any problem going to see a naturopath; in fact I preferred them over the legal drug-pushers that most medical doctors seemed to have become of late. It was more of a financial thing. There was the cost of the new patient visit and exam, and then if they wanted to do any specialized testing that would tack on another hefty fee, plus the cost of any supplements they recommended … By the time they were finished, you would walk out in a daze wondering where that five hundred dollars had just gone.

"Just remember, the longer you procrastinate, the more uncomfortable you may become," Mom reminded me. I grimaced at the memory her words evoked. I'd once had a very unfortunate episode when I was younger.

Since it involved intimate body functions I had chosen to keep the discomfort to myself until it had worsened into unbearable pain. The resultant exam and treatment was incredibly embarrassing, the whole experience made worse by discovering that it could've easily and quickly been resolved if I'd mentioned it when things first went awry.

"I know," I admitted. "Well I'd better get off to work, Mom, I've got a busy day ahead of me," I said, getting up off the sofa and grabbing my wallet from the coffee table.

"Oh that reminds me, Travis called the other day."

"Really? What about?" I asked. Funny that my Mom, living 3,000 miles away, had spoken to my roommate more recently than I had.

"Well he told me about the product you guys have started selling and he said he wanted to check and see if I would to buy some at your special discount. That's why I called you the other day, I thought it better if I bought it from you directly even though you're a team and all," she audibly smiled into the receiver. "So when you have a moment to really talk with me, go ahead and give me a call and we'll chat all about it." I frowned.

"I'm not selling anything with Travis," I said, a little more firmly than I had meant to.

"Oh aren't you? He told me that you two were trying to make some extra money and you were starting some sort of distribution something or other," she answered. "I could've been wrong, your Dad was watching Star Trek re-runs and I could barely hear myself think." I smiled. My Dad hated interruptions while he was watching TV.

He had learned that since it was impossible for my mom to stay entirely quiet for a whole half hour at a time, if he blasted the sound loud enough he couldn't hear anything but his show. Unfortunately, neither could anyone else. I shrugged it off, figuring Mom must have misunderstood something, whether it was the real caller's identity or the purpose of Travis' call. Still, it was strange if he had called her, whatever the reason. I would have to ask him about that.

"Okay, Mom. I gotta go," I pulled open the front door, and stepped out into the humid air. "I love you," I finished.

"Oh! Pirates!" my Mom suddenly said. "That's what your dreams were always about – pirates! How could I possibly forget that? You practically *were* a pirate when you were younger ..." her voice trailed off for a moment before coming back. "You would wake up in a terrible sweat, crying about being killed by pirates. Poor dear, you were so very frightened. It kept happening over and over and over again until we finally prohibited you from watching any pirate movies for a while, and then it went away. So very strange..."

Chapter 15

"No ma'am. I'm sorry ma'am. Yes ma'am," I dropped the phone back into the cradle and sighed, rubbing my forehead.

"Not interested?" Sophie smiled, patting my shoulder before starting her next call.

"Nope," I sighed again. The customer had not only been uninterested in the many timeshare opportunities I had to offer her, she had taken it upon herself to lecture me on just how rude it was to interrupt someone's dinner. It was 3:30 pm on a Wednesday afternoon; I hadn't realized it was dinnertime. Ironically, Sunriseset telemarketers were encouraged to work a later shift that included the dinner hour, simply because more people were at home during that time and you were therefore more likely to get someone to answer. I found it a prime time to see just how many expletives could be crammed into one angry sentence. The record was ten, so far. Apparently baby back ribs were ruined when you had to wipe your hands clean and answer the phone. Impulsively, I had said "Then why did you even bother to answer your phone?!" slammed the phone down, and then looked around to make sure no one had heard me. Luckily for me, it was exceptionally loud in the office at the time and my voice had been drowned out by all the other chatter. The only other concern I had was the quality control monitors who listened in on random calls – but one glance to their corner of the room found them enjoying a break with some peanut brittle and plenty of gossip. I had dodged the bullet, but my sudden impulsiveness still had me nervous and jittery.

I was on my last day of the two-week probationary period, and I had barely closed two deals in the last ten work days. Even those two I probably would have lost if Sophie hadn't jumped in and salvaged them for me at the last moment. "The end of the sale is always the hardest part," she reminded me. "They are interested and obviously have the financial means to move forward, they just need you to convince them that this is really *the* investment they are waiting for." I just smiled and nodded. I'd read the entire sales log to them – what more could I say? "Come on – stop farting around and just buy the damn timeshare already!" Oh yes, that was good. Emily Post, eat your heart out.

I found myself feeling anxious because my future at Sunriseset didn't look very good. Two deals in two weeks was not enough action to remain on the payroll. I was faced with the horror of actually having to *try*, or of looking for an entirely new job. Another glance up at the clock confirmed that it was time to take a break. I stood up, pushed my chair back and gesticulated to Sophie that I was going outside. She nodded and then rolled her eyes, the universal symbol for a troublesome caller. It was probably one of those individuals who would act interested and ask you a million questions, only to give you the "Well let me think about it." line at the end. They were probably just bored and glad to have someone to talk to, but not really interested at all in timeshares. Or anything else you could try and sell them.

I walked out of the back of the building and onto the small lawn that faced the Gulf. The water was very calm and glassy. It created a strange effect, looking more like a broad expanse of solid matter rather than a fluid ocean. A pelican flew across the water and dropped the remnants of a fish from his bill, disturbing the surface with a ripple that grew and grew, until gentle waves were lapping up against the sea wall just below me. I walked over to a vacant picnic table and sat down, leaning backwards and closing my eyes. The warmth of the sun was immediate, heating my face and my clothes. *I could fall asleep like this*, I thought to myself. As if sensing my relaxation a figure approached, standing over me and blocking out the sun. I frowned.

"Hey," Travis' voice was loud. I opened my eyes, squinting up at his face.

"Hey," I responded. After a long enough pause to ensure he wasn't going to offer the answer on his own, I asked, "What're you doing here?"

"Had a delivery in the area, figured I'd stop by. You said they had a nice break room so I thought I'd check it out," Travis sat down beside me and leaned back as I had done. Two female coworkers approached us, jabbering about some vacation one of them was planning. They were like chickadees, chirping in excitement as details were spilled. Travis and I watched them for a few minutes as they passed us and continued along on their walk.

"Got any pizza?" I asked. I wasn't particularly hungry, but I also wouldn't pass up an opportunity to have some of Ruth's specialty pizza.

"Nah, I'm done for the day," Travis answered as he closed his eyes.

"Damn," I swore quietly. The words sunk in and I glanced over at Travis. "Really—you're done for the day? At four in the afternoon?" Travis shifted slightly on the bench.

"Yeah, they closed early today. Some family thing," Travis explained.

"Huh," I answered, once again reclining and closing my eyes. "Hey – did you call my Mom the other day?" I asked, sitting up and turning toward him again.

"Yeah," Travis admitted easily.

"Why?"

"I was looking for your number, and when I couldn't find it, I called her to ask for it."

"Oh," that seemed simple enough. But then, "You don't remember my number but you know my mom's?"

"It's taped to the fridge door," Travis responded immediately

Oh yeah. "Did you try to sell her something?"

"Yeah, it was a joke. When she first answered the phone I pretended it was a sales call, and she immediately went to hang up on me so I told her who I was. I guess she didn't figure it was a joke, and assumed that I really was selling the product." Travis chuckled.

"Sounds like Mom," I confirmed. It wasn't too much fun to play jokes when they were taken seriously; it always ruined the punchline and deflated the ego. I'd stopped trying to joke with my Mom years ago for that very reason.

"I'm going down to the Keys this weekend," Travis said casually. I rolled my head to the side and squinted at him.

"The Keys?"

"Yeah, one of the guys at work is getting married in a couple of weeks. He's having his bachelor blowout down there this weekend, and he invited me."

"To the Keys?" I asked again. Travis opened his eyes and frowned at me, his "You stupid?" look.

"Yeah, the Keys. He's a fishing nut and apparently there's some real good fishing down there – about 30 miles east of Key West near some little island…Markis? Marsan? Anyway, his future father-in-law has a nice yacht that's docked down in Key West, and is taking him fishing for his bachelor party."

"And you're invited?" I asked, before leaning back and closing my eyes again.

"Pretty weird, yeah. I guess he doesn't have that many friends around here and he really wanted to fill the boat, so he just started throwing out some random invitations..." Travis shrugged and the bench moved slightly.

"Well jeeze, that's nice. I like Ruth's Pizza, can I come?" I asked, only partly joking. I was serious about wanting to take a trip down to the Keys, not so serious about inviting myself to a stranger's bachelor party ritual. At least at this one there probably wouldn't be any strippers.

"I don't think so, man. He said today that the boat's finally full," Travis sounded nervous, like he'd inadvertently given an implied invitation that may cause his own to be rescinded. I shrugged.

"Too bad. Could be nice you know," I paused, rubbing my chin thoughtfully, "To get away for a weekend like that."

"Yeah," Travis acknowledged emptily. "Not that it'll be too exciting or anything. He's kinda a geek, so his friends will likely be pencil pushers. There certainly won't be any strippers or anything. There may not even be any booze, but then I have no idea what we'll do. Unless we really are just fishing. From what I hear, the islands are completely off-limits – some kinda government preservation thing."

"In the Keys?" I asked, frowning a little and feeling that the sun was already burning the furrows across my forehead. "Doesn't everybody drive across bridges from key to key down there anyway?

"Yeah, but these ones are further southwest of Key West, beyond the bridges. There's a few of them that are like that – special or something. The Markies – The Marquesas Keys. That's it," Travis sighed.

"Huh," I answered. Suddenly the sun felt very warm on my chest, and the delicious sensation of oncoming sleep dulled my senses. "Sounds nice," I slurred, closing my eyes.

"CJ?" Travis' voice was distant and muted.

"Mmmm?" I responded, reluctant to force off the wonderful warmth that flowed through every limb–from the top of my head to the tips of my fingers and toes.

"Are you okay?" Travis' voice pushed through the edges of my consciousness, more urgent now.

"Mmmmm…" I responded, only slightly curious about why my perfectly-formed "yes" came out sounding so muffled.

"CJ!" The alarm in Travis' voice was plain, but I felt wonderfully disconnected and unconcerned. I relaxed, giving in and drifting off to sleep.

***

The slave stood before the crew, dripping wet, his eyes huge as he tried to catch his breath.

"Did you see her?" Alamar shoved past the others, towering over the small, scrawny man. The slave nodded.

"Can you reach her?" Duarte asked, looking grimly into the dark waves.

"Barely," the slave puffed, still desperate to catch his breath.

"What about the cargo hold?" Alamar asked urgently, spitting flecks of foamy spittle onto the slave. The slave shook his head, sending water drops cascading onto the deck.

"It's too far. The hatches are shut," the slave shrugged helplessly. There were a few moments of silence, and only the creaking of the ship and the wind blowing through the rigging could be heard. The greed in Duarte's heart once again receded and was replaced by fear.

"It's no use if we can't breach the cargo hold," Duarte muttered. "We should fall back." Alamar turned, his eyes fierce and burning.

"We aren't finished yet," Alamar's voice was low and urgent.

"But if they can't breathe long enough to enter the hold…" Duarte stopped, leaving the obvious unsaid.

"Then we need to find them more air," Alamar said simply. He paused for a moment, thinking. Suddenly, his countenance brightened. "Master Rosales," he turned and looked toward a member of the crew who stepped forward eagerly. Rosales was one of the few who had welcomed the mutiny and willingly obeyed Alamar's every order. "Retrieve the iron pot from the Captain's Quarters." Rosales nodded with a soft "Aye" and disappeared. A few moments later he returned, a large iron pot in his arms. Alamar nodded, waving at the deck, and Rosales put the pot down. Alamar looked at Duarte and pointed to the pot, "More air." Duarte shook his head, frowning in disbelief.

"The pot?"

"Yes, a pot this way. More air," Alamar lifted the pot and turned it over, raising his hand into the empty space inside, "This way. The iron will lend weight for the descent, and then when the lungs are empty, the pot will grant another breath of air and allow the slaves to enter the hold." Alamar placed the pot back onto the deck. Duarte's heart leapt forward again, his hopes renewed.

"Are there others?" Duarte asked eagerly. Alamar shook his head.

"The Captain had the foresight to believe it might garner a fine fee with the merchants back home, but he also had the shortcoming to consider it a risk and therefore brought only one. Always of little faith—the least of his mistakes," his eyes drifted to the open sea as his mind wandered. A moment later he was back and barking orders. "Rosales, bring some rope! Covas, netting! Vega, iron shot from the cannons!"

Within minutes the supplies had been placed on the deck at Alamar's feet. The crew worked to his directions, securing the rope and netting to the pot. The bosun barked orders and two crewmen scaled the rigging, carrying the rope with them and looping it over the yardarm before dropping it back to the deck. Alamar indicated to two crewmen on deck, who lifted the rope and then heaved, raising the pot into the air. The netting hung low on either sides of the pot, heavy with iron shot to steady it as it sank into the depths. The slaves watched in horror as the makeshift life support system that was meant *to sustain them on the ocean floor was lowered into the water. Alamar turned, his eyes wild.*

"You!" he indicated to a slave that stood trembling on the deck. The slave moved forward slowly, cowering away from Alamar's tall frame. "Bring me some treasure," Alamar sneered. The slave shook, stepping to the rail and lowering himself into the water. He expanded his lungs with a deep breath of air, perhaps the last he'd ever breathe, and disappeared beneath the surface.

As the pot and slave descended into the watery depths, Alamar turned to Duarte, a crazy fire burning in his eyes. Duarte shivered and turned away.

"CJ?" a hand patted my shoulder. "CJ, are you okay? Christopher?" another pat, harder this time. I opened my eyes to find Sophie and about fifteen other Sunriseset employees standing over me. I started to sit up, but Sophie shook her head, pushing me back.

"What's going on?" I asked, raising my hand to shield my eyes from the sunlight that shone directly into my face. Someone shifted, and their shadow fell over me.

"That's what I wanna know," Sophie said, pressing a cool, wet cloth to my forehead. "You fainted," she added.

"Passed out," someone else corrected.

"Sorry, passed out," Sophie said.

"Passed out?" I asked, trying to focus on the crowd around me. They looked more interested than concerned for my situation, whatever it may be.

"Yeah. A couple people saw you lounging on the bench and then you just sort of..." Sophie patted my forehead with the cloth as she paused to find the right words, "Keeled over." I shook my head and laughed.

"Nah, I just fell asleep. I'm fine," I said, trying once again to sit up. This time Sophie didn't stop me, and in fact put an encouraging hand under my back as I leaned forward. Several of the onlookers dispersed, uninterested in me now that my situation was apparently unremarkable. A few stayed behind and one woman leaned down, her auburn hair falling forward across her face and into mine.

"Are you sure?" she asked, her breath washing over me. It smelled refreshingly of something sweet – perhaps a fruity lifesaver? "You slid over and really hit the bench hard there. Most people would've woken up when that happened."

"Yeah, I'm sure," I said, pushing myself up onto my feet. She smiled, exposing beautiful porcelain caps, and then turned away. The last few onlookers turned with her, moving away and leaving me alone with Sophie. Sophie smiled warmly at me, and once again patted my arm.

"You really fall asleep hard, don't ya?" she asked. I nodded. "Well I'd better get back in. They called me out to check on you when you wouldn't respond, I'm first aid and CPR trained and they were about to call an ambulance. I'm just glad you're okay. But you may wanna put something on that bump, it's pretty swollen."

"Yeah, thanks," I shrugged. "I'll be back in shortly, just gonna take a moment."

"Good idea. I'll see you inside."

As I watched Sophie walk away, a dull twinge on the left side of my forehead caused me to raise my hand and rub my head. "Ow!" I sucked in my breath as my hand contacted a tender spot that had swelled to the size of a grape. As I tried to review what had happened, I realized that Travis was nowhere around. "Huh," I muttered quietly, tenderly rubbing my head as I walked back into the office.

I didn't want to admit what had just happened—even to myself. Maybe if I ignored it, things would just go back to normal. But even I knew that was a lie. *Better that than the truth*, I counseled myself. *Now I was suffering nightmares in middle of the day?*

Chapter 16

Thanks to Sophie's recommendation to the "higher ups", Sunriseset allowed me to leave early that day. I decided to stop by the library and use the Internet. After a brief search through the online yellow pages I found a local nutritionist who promised he would go easy on the billing. Lucky for me he had an available appointment that very afternoon; someone else had cancelled and left a vacancy. I left my name with the receptionist and got directions to the office. The office was set back in a residential area, about five blocks off the closest bus routes, but I figured the walk would do me good.

The doctor's office was also his home, a small two-story house on a nice lot that was halfway down a dead-end street. The first floor foyer had been turned into a waiting room with an assortment of armchairs and bookshelves to make oneself comfortable with. What had probably been a small spare bedroom was now the receptionist's corner, with a small peek-through window cut into the wall. I glanced around at the other patients, reclining comfortably with the latest gossip or sports magazines. I, however, was not so lucky, being given a virtual tome of forms to fill out. Did it really matter if my grandfather's uncle had heart disease? Apparently it did, so I checked "No". I made my way down the rest of the forms, skipping questions that were irrelevant (like when my last menstruation was) and handing the whole thing back to the receptionist. She smiled up at me and indicated toward an empty chair.

"Please have a seat, the doctor will be right with you." I nodded and sat down, wondering what "Right with you" meant at this particular practice. Five minutes? Fifteen? I found an issue of Sports Illustrated on the bookshelf next to me and picked it up, just to have something to do.

Twenty minutes later a woman stepped into the waiting area. "Mr. Durbrin?" she glanced around the room, smiling at me when I nodded and raised my arm. "Please come this way," she waited for me to step before her into a small hallway, before indicating to a door on my right. "In here, please," she said, pushing the door open and stepping through behind me.

The room was another converted bedroom, the closet holding an array of supplements on shelves instead of clothing on rails. A small fish tank, filled with colorful guppies, sat on a stand in the corner, offering a welcome sight for anyone who was resigned to wait in the room for more than a few minutes. There was a small desk, also loaded with various supplements, and a shelf next to the table held some various decorative trinkets. A long chiropractic table was placed in the center of the room, and I took a seat on it. The woman smiled at me again.

"The doctor will be right in," she placed my tome of forms on the table and stepped out of the room, closing the door behind her. I sighed, wondering what the purpose of appointment times were. I glanced over the various plaques on the wall, reading the many degrees and qualifications of the nutritionist I was about to see. Another ten minutes had passed before the door opened and the nutritionist stepped into the room.

Dr. Albert Poll was a tall man, with dark brown hair and an impressive jaw line. He wore an official-looking white coat and carried a clipboard, to which he clipped my papers before he stepped up to me, his arm extended.

"Hello Christopher, I'm Dr. Poll," he shook my hand firmly, turning his attention to my paperwork. "What brings you in?" he asked.

"I've been having some trouble sleeping lately," I answered.

"What kind of trouble?" Dr. Poll looked at me and furrowed his brow, his pen poised to take down whatever I said that he considered to be important.

"Well I've been having vivid dreams, a little more vivid than normal," I explained.

"How's your diet?" Dr. Poll asked, his eyes returning to the paperwork I had filled out. I grimaced. "Do you eat three meals a day?" Dr. Poll asked. I nodded. "Vegetables every day?" I frowned. "Take any vitamins right now?" I shook my head. "Do you drink alcohol? Smoke?" I shook my head again. "Alright. Well let's see what's going on. Go ahead and lie down here," he pulled a fresh sheet of paper across the headrest of the table. I laid back, my head crinkling the paper. "Have you ever had muscle testing before?" Dr. Poll asked, as he turned and placed his clipboard on his desk. I nodded.

"A few times. My Mom swears by it," I answered.

"Good, then you know how it works. I want you to raise your right arm, here," he held his hand against my wrist, "And I want you to match my pressure." He pushed and I held my arm steady. "Good. I'm just going to check your basic body systems," he quickly pointed his right index finger over various areas of my body from my forehead down to my hips, pushing against my arm with his right hand each time. I matched his pressure, my hand holding firm. "Well everything looks good here, let me check some irritants," he held a box full of small, liquid-filled vials over my stomach and pushed against my arm. Another box, another push, and then again and yet again. After the fifth time he set the last box down on his desk and turned to me.

"You can put you arm down, and sit up," Dr. Poll took a seat in the small swivel chair that had been hidden under his desk.

"So?" I asked.

"Well, though I would like to see you improve your diet habits and eat more nutritiously, the fact is that your body is testing as fine," Dr. Poll answered. "It's not testing that you are deficient or fighting against anything."

"So ..." I asked, shrugging my shoulders.

"I don't see any nutritional reason why you would be having sleep-interrupting dreams — now are they dreams or nightmares?" he asked.

"Just dreams," I lied. "They're really vivid though," I added.

"Huh," Dr. Poll looked puzzled. Apparently all those plaques on the wall didn't equal a know-it-all. "Well I'd consider getting some vitamin B-1 and B-Complex and take about 100 milligrams just before you go to bed, see if that helps. You can also take long walks, preferably barefoot on the earth, shortly before going to bed each night. This should help your body relax and absorb the natural cues that contribute to deep, restorative sleep."

"Thanks," I said, though I didn't really mean it. I felt cheated, paying for an opinion that didn't actually help me resolve the issues I had come in for.

"You're welcome. Darlene can set you up with some B-1 and B-Complex if you'd like. And feel free to call if anything changes," he shook my hand again and stepped out of the office.

"Well damn," I swore as soon as the door had closed. To say that I was disappointed would've been seriously understating the situation. I'd never visited a nutritionist before who hadn't found at least one thing to handle regarding my health. It was usually my kidneys, my liver, my gallbladder, or something else connected to my digestive system. Even if I didn't believe in nutrition as wholeheartedly as my mom did, it made sense to me that poor digestion could lead to poor quality sleep. I glanced around the room once more, at the plaques on the wall and the supplements in the closet. I stepped over to the door and pulled it open.

Back to the drawing board.

Chapter 17

I awoke late on Saturday morning, and found myself confronting a weekend alone at the house while Travis was off carousing with his new friends in the Keys. I felt like a shunned lover – passed over when a more interesting opportunity presented itself. After sulking around the house until noon, I decided to drown my sorrows in another trip to the beach. It was an idiotic choice to make that late in the day, but I had purposely drawn out my suffering and now I could either continue to sulk or spend a few hours out of the house, doing something different. I opted for the latter.

As I neared the bus stop closest to our house, I realized that I was once again five minutes late for the last bus and twenty-five minutes early for the next one. As if to confirm this, the traffic on the road in front of me suddenly dissolved away, revealing the rear of the bus that I'd just barely missed. I sighed, a rather pitiful sound, and weighed my options. I decided to walk south along Alternate 19, and catch the next bus at a stop further down. Not five minutes later, as I approached the next stop, the sun had beaten me into submission and I sank onto the bench. Sweat had beaded on my forehead, rolling into and stinging my eyes. I grabbed the corner of my towel out of my bag and rubbed it across my face, only succeeding in temporarily drying it.

The bus stop bench was placed at the base of a tree, probably in the hopes that it would be kept somewhat cooler by the tree's shade. However, due to the tree's interesting and wind-battered shape, the only shade the tree offered was thrown five feet west of the bench, across the sidewalk and into someone's front yard. There, on what passed for grass in this part of the country, sat a homeless man who was having a very heated discussion with himself. Having nothing better to do while I waited for the next bus, I angled my body sideways on the bench so that I could glimpse the homeless man to my right without ogling him too openly and obviously.

What at first seemed to be complete gibberish slowly began to make sense as I listened. Although it was clearly out of place, the man was discussing the virtues of an alternative tax system, rubbing and folding between his hands what might have once been a hat. As I continued to watch him, I realized there was no real reason, aside from the conversation with himself, to assume the man was homeless. He was not particularly dirty, and while his jeans looked worn, some of my own favorite pairs of jeans had far more holes. His shirt was unwrinkled and his hair windblown, but not particularly long or untidy. He definitely appeared nervous and a bit out of sorts, but perhaps he was preparing for his public speaking debut and was working himself up to the challenge. I inched myself closer so as to better hear his arguments, but my bus suddenly arrived out of nowhere, hissing to a stop along the curb. I glanced down at my phone, thumbing the side tab to bring up the screen, and saw from the time that twenty minutes had passed.

I stood up and boarded the bus, nodding to the driver as I showed him my monthly pass and made my way back to an empty seat. Against all odds the bus was only half-full and I was able to set my backpack on the seat next to me. My mumbling friend had boarded just behind me, and as he approached my seat he looked me squarely in the eyes and spoke clearly before continuing past.

"Never mind what you can see, it's what you can't see that is most troublesome."

I nodded absently and he moved down the aisle. A voice inside told me that whatever was going on with that man had absolutely nothing to do with me, and I shouldn't waste even one second worrying about it. A deeper voice, one that terrified me to my very core, told me that I should listen, because the man was absolutely right.

***

It was the fifth haul on the net, and the fifth time Duarte had felt chills down his spine. The silver bars looked bigger than he had remembered as they were removed from the net and placed on deck. Alamar stood protectively over them, like a mother bear guarding her cubs. He was just as big, and definitely just as dangerous. A slave surfaced in the waves just off the starboard side, immediately followed by another, indicating that their artificial air supply was exhausted. The men on deck hauled on the line, pulling the iron pot to the surface. Duarte turned to Alamar, who had not moved from his position over the bars.

"Aren't they beautiful?" his voice dripped with greed and his eyes were unmoving. Duarte nodded, his eyes also fixed on the treasure they had freed from the ocean's watery grip.

"We haven't much time, we should retrieve some of the gems," Duarte suggested. Though sharp lookouts had yet to see white sails on the horizon, the fear of capture still haunted him. Alamar shook his head.

"The silver will fetch a fine price."

"Perhaps, but the silver is recorded," Duarte indicated markings on the bars, "And it will be missed."

"And the blame will be laid upon the scribe or the sea," Alamar said, raising his eyes at last. The fiery flame in them had grown stronger, and Duarte could not hold his gaze.

"Perhaps it is time we find a place to hide the silver until it is safe to recover," Duarte offered, raising his eyes to Alamar's chin and no higher. Alamar smiled.

"Yes Duarte, tend to your maps and find our treasure a safe haven," Alamar waved his arm, sending Duarte away.

Duarte retreated to the ship's cabin and poured himself over the array of charts heaped on the navigational table. They were surrounded by a plentiful assortment of low-lying islands, any of which would've likely served well as their cache. His eyes fell on a group of islands shaped like a tilted horseshoe that lay just to the west of them. It seemed perfect, but was it too obvious? Duarte shook his head, running his hand along the map. To the east was another set of scattered islands, smaller and perhaps less obvious. But wait, Duarte reasoned silently, if it seemed obvious to him, it may also seem obvious to others. It followed then, that the most obvious location was actually the safest location. Duarte traced his finger lightly on the map, finding a route to the northernmost and largest landmass in the horseshoe islands. It was here, he decided, that they would hide their treasure.

Duarte smiled, pulling a fresh sheet of cloth onto the table and beginning to draw the map. As the first drop of ink stained the cloth he was stopped dead by an angry growl from Alamar. The words were not discernible, but clearly he was cursing someone on deck. Duarte's blood ran cold as he reviewed their actions, and once again called into question the character of the man he was serving. If greed could turn an honest man into a pirate and murderer, what was to stop him there? With the silver safely stored in its cache, Alamar had every reason to take the necessary steps that would secure it all for himself.

Fear gave way to anger as Duarte envisioned the slaughter that most assuredly awaited all on-board this ship, himself included. He grasped the only weapon he had and fiercely began to use it, his hand shaking in fear of the deception it wrought.

"End of the line!" the bus driver's loud call forced me awake. I sat up in my seat, immediately conscious of the puddle of drool on my cheek. I rubbed my arm across my face as I adjusted to my surroundings. I had missed my stop at the beach, riding the bus to the end of the line for the route. Those who wanted to remain on the bus were forced to disembark and cross the center median of the station before re-boarding, a charade designed by someone who surely had nothing better to do than think up schemes to make the simplest tasks a little more complicated. Still woozy from my unexpected nap, I grabbed my bag and stumbled off the bus.

As I stood yawning on the sidewalk, the man I'd once thought was homeless strolled up to me. A smile lit his lips as he stared into my eyes and opened his mouth to impart some final wisdom.

"Don't you see?" he asked, his eyes dancing with laughter as he moved away.

I stood completely still as I watched him move away, an involuntary shiver running down my spine.

Chapter 18

Another week passed and found me still holding down a job. Somehow I had managed to close five deals just in time to stay on board at Sunriseset. Sophie, ever proud of her successful trainees, invited me to a celebration dinner at our neighboring Chinese Restaurant on Friday evening. I felt as giddy as a teenage boy going on a first date, even though it was hardly an exclusive evening. Three of Sophie's other trainees had also made the grade and were joining us, along with an assortment of various other coworkers... and Sophie's fiancee. To prove (to myself, mostly) that I understood the casualness of the evening (or perhaps just to soften the blow to my wounded heart and pride), I invited Travis along. After first making sure there was nothing of interest on television that evening, he agreed and showed up just as we were being seated.

A few people tried to start a full-on introduction around the table, but there were too many independent conversations going on and it was finally abandoned after the fourth attempt. Those that were curious simply resolved the matter one-on-one with the individuals they didn't know. As orders were taken and delivered to the kitchen, Travis the entertainer helped pass the time by telling jokes – most of them of a questionable nature when it came to being politically correct. His audience was unconcerned, however, and laughed all the harder at the more inane comments.

The food arrived a good hour after the orders were placed, and the meals were distributed by what looked to be the restaurant's entire wait staff. Conversation continued, but in smaller groups as everyone started in on their meals. I'm not exactly sure how it happened, but a casual conversation about the highlights of Travis' recent trip to the Keys turned into a heated debate with a coworker of mine who was seated to Travis' left. Travis was arguing the seemingly arbitrary system that the government used to designate new wildlife preserves. From the sounds of it, he was taking it personally that the government's power extended into the area of making parts of the United States off limits to civilians whenever they pleased. His opponent, a well-fed man dressed in a loud Hawaiian shirt and jean shorts, was calmly extolling the virtues of the government's wise decision to protect natural resources by labeling new preserves on a regular basis.

"I'm not saying I disagree with certain lands being protected, I'm saying that there should be more reason employed when designating new protected zones," Travis argued around a mouthful of Kung Pao shrimp. Hawaii shook his head. I dug into my Mu Shu chicken wraps, savoring the hoisin sauce I generously spooned over them, and otherwise keeping my mouth shut.

"The primary reason seems to be consideration for the wildlife and natural vegetation present there," Hawaii argued. "That sounds like reason enough."

"I understand that, but the rules are still arbitrary," Travis swallowed. Hawaii shook his head again. "Okay look," Travis began to explain himself, "If man moves in to populate an area that is ripe with natural vegetation and wildlife and his presence encroaches upon that, it is a fair argument that such areas should be protected. However, if man creates a place that is untouched by any wildlife and only *after* human involvement does wildlife seek out and populate that place, it follows that man is the one who has been encroached upon." Hawaii stared, dumbfounded. I didn't blame him since I too had been lost. Travis continued, "Like the islands along the waterway here – you know the ones I'm talking about?" Hawaii nodded. "Those were manmade islands, created by the sand that was dredged up out of the channel. Over time, vegetation has grown up on the islands and wildlife has followed, populating them."

"Yeah," Hawaii said in agreement.

"So once they reach a certain level of vegetation and population, the man-made islands are designated as wildlife preserves and therefore off-limits to the very men who put them there in the first place."

"Uh-huh," Hawaii seemed to be waiting for some sort of point that had yet to be made. I was too. "So?"

"Well what if a man takes his girlfriend for a romantic little sailing trip and decides to anchor near one of these still publicly-accessible islands. They go ashore for a nice little picnic where he proceeds to romance her off her feet and then proposes to her," another bite of Kung Pao shrimp. "Five years later they come back on vacation, intending to relive the magic of the day he proposed, only to discover that they aren't allowed on their little island because now it's a wildlife sanctuary. Not wanting to waste their whole trip, they sneak ashore anyway and are promptly arrested and fined. Is that really fair?" Travis implored Hawaii, who had long since stopped eating and was just staring in wonderment. I myself wondered what Travis was really getting at—he didn't seem to be one who would argue about the government's designation of wildlife preserves.

"Well now, the thing to remember is," Hawaii sought for his footing to make a good argument, "We have taken so much land from wildlife over our years here, that if they take some back from us, it's only fair and our duty to relinquish it." I smiled, it was a fine rebuttal.

"I think it's horseshit," Travis said. Hawaii smiled, and I'm sure he shared my thought that the expletive seemed to indicate that Travis was conceding defeat.

"I guess the question really is — are you yourself planning a trip that was been thwarted by one of these wildlife designations?" Hawaii asked. Travis shrugged, shaking his head.

"That's beside the point," Travis argued, just as it dawned on me that this was exactly his point. "If man has put something somewhere legally, the federal government has no business rescinding his right to the land, or the property."

"You have property on one of the waterway islands?" Hawaii asked, raising an eyebrow.

"No," Travis said firmly, frustrated. "I'm just trying to make a point here."

"I dunno," Hawaii said airily, "It sounds to me like it's more of a personal vendetta than just a point. I honestly don't think anyone else has a problem with the abundance of wildlife preserves around the country, regardless of any emotional attachment to them. And the government doesn't always place the land in a preserve completely off-limits to civilians. I mean look at Yosemite, Yellowstone, the Grand Canyon."

"That's my point," Travis argued. "Why can they decide to restrict some and not others? I mean, why is a little waterway island more valuable than the Grand Canyon? What do you think...CJ?" He suddenly turned toward me, and for a second all time stopped. The pause between the question and my name hadn't been deliberate—it had been the sort of obvious pause that occurs when someone forgets the name of the individual they are addressing. But there was more to it, and it was horribly familiar.

The restaurant dissolved around us, all sounds were muted and the air grew still. I saw before me someone I simultaneously didn't recognize and yet knew all too well. The crushing truth of who he was–of who I was–chilled my blood and my eyes drifted involuntarily to the knife on the table, hidden just below Travis' hand. As his fingers curled around the silver handle, mine curled around air in response. My mind raced, as I struggled to understand what was happening. It felt familiar, like a dream, but with an additional element I couldn't quite put my finger on. It almost seemed like...but no, it couldn't be the past, because then that would mean...

Suddenly, Travis began to laugh. The sights and sounds of the restaurant returned all at once, and I felt shaken and weak.

"Good god, man, it's not that serious!" Travis squeezed out in between loud guffaws. I frowned, and Travis only laughed harder, pointing at my face. I felt the tear roll down my cheek and shrugged, nonchalantly wiping it away from my face with a half-smile.

"You know me, a good argument always makes me cry," I said halfheartedly, feeling my heart beating hard in my throat. Travis turned away from me and the moment passed, leaving only a lingering whisper of a feeling in its wake.

***

After a good two hours at the table, the party finally came to a close. The waiters seemed to sense it, and rushed over with the check. Somehow the request for separate checks (about fourteen of them) had been denied, and we were forced to figure out the math on our own. Travis threw some money onto the table and excused himself, heading off toward the bathroom. The check slowly made its way around the table to me, and I struggled to divvy up my portion despite the dim lighting and distracting noise. With taxes and eighteen percent gratuity, I somehow ended up shelling out almost double the cost of my meal. Even so, when all of the contributions were totaled we were still fifteen bucks short on the bill, and we all had to pitch in some more change to cover it. That meant that when all was said and done I had paid no less than eighteen bucks for my eight dollar meal. I began to wonder if there was some dishonesty afoot – either there was an inflated bill or someone had decided not to pay their full share. No one seemed interested in spending any more time on the matter, though, and I decided to chalk it up to a life lesson – never share a check with a bevy of strangers. Travis appeared just as everyone was leaving, and together we walked out to the bus stop for the long, boring ride home.

Chapter 19

I woke up early the next day and after ascertaining that the house was empty, I decided to go out in search of breakfast. By the time I got to the end of the street I'd lost interest in pursuing a decent meal, mostly because I was just too lazy to walk that far. I spotted the local liquor store, a sign in the window advertising Krispy Kreme donuts, and decided that this would suffice. After an indecisive moment in front of the display, I opened the plastic door and removed two original glazed donuts, dropping them into a paper bag. I grabbed a small bottle of orange juice out of the refrigerator and walked up to the counter.

"Morning," I said to the cashier as I pulled my wallet from my pocket.

"Three sixty-four," the cashier responded. I handed him a five dollar bill and he punched numbers into the cash register, stepping back as the drawer sprung open. He placed the change into my hand with a "Good day," and then conveniently forgot I existed as he turned his attention to the next customer. I grabbed my purchases and walked to the door, and then stopped and turned back to the newspaper rack. I scanned the front page, searching for whatever had grabbed my attention a moment before. After a few moments of finding nothing, I shrugged and was about to turn away once more when I saw it again and stopped, grabbing the paper and flipping back to the story.

"Hey, this is not a library," the cashier suddenly remembered my existence, glaring over the side of the counter at me.

"Sorry, how much for the paper?" I asked.

"Seventy-five cents," the cashier responded. I shoved the dollar from my change into his hand, tucking the paper under my arm and walking out the door. As I entered the house a few moments later I was greeted by the rather unusual sight of Travis standing over the stove, cooking.

"Hey – what do you think about a trip down to Miami?" Travis asked casually as he stirred his scrambled eggs.

"Hmm?" I asked, only half-listening to him. I self-consciously tucked the newspaper tighter against my body.

"Miami – haven't you ever thought about going down there?" Travis repeated, noisily scraping the eggs out of the pan and onto a plate.

"I dunno," I shrugged. "Didn't you just get back from a trip to the Keys?"

"Yeah – that's why I wanna go to Miami. I was just passing through, and it looked nice. Hell of a lot closer than the Keys, too," Travis stood, leaning against the kitchen counter as he shoveled eggs into his mouth. He paused to shake more salt onto them before continuing to shovel. "So what about it?" he asked, prying open a Coke and sipping loudly. What a combination – eggs and Coke. My stomach turned at the thought.

"How do you propose we get there?" I asked.

"My work car," Travis said casually, shoveling and sipping. I was suddenly reminded of the Monty Python skit where an incredibly large man ate an incredibly large meal and was asked if he wanted just one little dinner mint. My mind re-adjusted and I realized what Travis had said.

"You're going to steal your work car?" I asked. I felt the heat of anger rising in my throat and to my face.

"No, I'm not gonna steal my work car," Travis cut across my internal rant and I felt momentarily rebuffed. "I asked them if I could borrow it for a trip, and they said sure, as long as I rotated the tires and got an oil change before I left."

"Well what about their deliveries?"

"Turns out they've been looking at getting a new delivery car for awhile; this one's pretty beaten up and it's not so good for business," Travis said, taking another sip of Coke and belching loudly. "They're buying a new one on Friday, which makes it perfect timing to borrow this one for the weekend and a few days beyond."

"Well do you think the car could actually make that trip?" I questioned. Although the idea of going down to Miami was interesting, the idea of being stranded on a highway in the Florida Everglades was *not* enticing. I'd heard stories about alligators crossing the highway down there. Big ones.

"It's only four hundred forty miles, the car has to have at least that much still left in it," Travis shrugged, scraping the rest of the eggs into his mouth and dumping the plate into the sink.

"What about gas?" I asked. At over three dollars a gallon most everywhere, gas prices had become a major concern to any American who had a car.

"Well that's the good part about this car. It does about thirty miles to a gallon, which makes this trip around fourteen and a half gallons each way, which is around sixty bucks each. That's not too bad," Travis reasoned.

"Yeah, but what about food, lodging, you know – all that stuff?" I was only mildly surprised to find that I actually did want to go, but I wasn't about to find out halfway down there that Travis' grand idea of solving financial difficulties consisted of begging on the side of the road when we'd run out of money.

"I've saved up about two hundred dollars in tips, and I figure you've got to have about that much yourself from work. We don't spend much here; we should be able to take a four-day trip down there. And hell, we can just park at the beach and sleep there. Forget a hotel," Travis shrugged.

"I've got the money. You want to go this weekend?" I asked, only mildly bothered by the lie I had just told.

"Yeah. Can you get off?"

"I don't know – they want two weeks notice for vacations," I didn't really care, I had decided that I would go anyway, even if it meant getting fired. The idea of not seeing Sophie every day was a little disheartening, but the fact was that Sunriseset was below the level of manageable monotony, even for me, and I was pretty sure I wouldn't last another month there.

"So don't tell them you're going, and just call in sick with the flu on Friday. That will hold you through the next week, and they won't know the difference." That was Travis – if it got you what you wanted, a lie wasn't actually a bad thing at all. I tried to console myself with the idea that I had lied before I met him, and that it wasn't something he had forced me into.

"Fine, I'll go," I said, turning around and heading for my bedroom.

I tossed the newspaper onto the bed and then picked it back up again, flipping to the story that had caught my attention. It outlined details of a twenty-one year old college student, whose bank account had been wiped out in what officials were calling an ingenious robbery scam. The money had just been deposited the day before by her grandparents, and it was for her upcoming tuition payments for her senior year. The story reported that a young man had contacted her over the phone, and with some convincing details about her personal life that very few people knew, he managed to convince her that he was one of her grandparents' employees. There had been an error on the deposits, and her tuition payment would be short unless he was able to deposit more money. It was the oldest scam in the book but she fell for it, relinquishing her bank routing and account numbers so that the problem could be rectified. Of course now she really *did* have a problem making the tuition payment, since every single dime had been drained from the account. It was only after it happened that she realized the irony; if the man really *had* worked for her grandparents, he would've had her bank information from them. Unfortunately, in moments of panic and fear, most individuals acted irrationally, something the perpetrators of scams counted on. The victim told reporters that the man had been such a smooth talker that she really hadn't considered the sheer illogic of his requests—and he had seemed so genuine and knew so much about her that she truly believed he must work for her grandparents.

The story ended with the victim's identifying details. Her name was Lucy Bolzen – she was the granddaughter of William and Ruth Bolzen and the brainchild behind Ruth's Pizza.

Chapter 20

The next day at work, after wrestling with a particularly disgruntled gentleman who decidedly had never expressed interest in purchasing a timeshare and wanted my name and employee number so he could "report me to the authorities," I decided it was time for a break. The air-conditioning unit for the office was on the fritz, making the air both humid and stale. A variety of colognes and perfumes, mostly cheap ones, had mixed with body odor and sweat to form a disagreeably pungent odor that was likely to blame for the sinus headache I now suffered from. I grabbed a pad of paper and a pen, and walked out back.

Though both the humidity and the temperature were slightly higher outside, the fresh ocean breeze cleared my head and opened my sinuses. As I sat on the picnic bench and breathed in the salty sea air, my thoughts turned to the upcoming trip to Miami and I willed the day to move faster and be over. After a moment I sighed and pulled my cell phone from my pocket. Embarrassing though it was, being incredibly outdated and therefore huge, it was still a cell phone and it connected me with the one person who just might be able to help me out.

"Hi Mom," I said into the phone as soon as the connection clicked through. I'd placed the pad onto the picnic table and started doodling, a habit that had recently become almost obsessive. Some people would write their name again and again and others would draw little pictures–I always drew a sort of lopsided circle of disconnected shapes on the paper. I didn't know why, I'd just started doing it. I reasoned it was a better habit than smoking, and it kept my hand busy while I was on the phone.

"Hi Honey!! I was just thinking about you!" my Mom sang into the phone. I couldn't help but smile, despite the new helping of guilt she had just managed to pour on without even realizing it.

"How are you?" I asked, having decided that if I were a little more conversational from the get-go, it wouldn't be so bad that I had only thought to call because I needed something from her.

"I'm doing fine, sweetheart. Your timing is perfect; I was just coming in for a moment to get some iced tea before going back out into the garden. Did I tell you what your Dad gave me for our anniversary?" it was so innocent, but her comment still managed to press the guilt button. I'd forgotten their anniversary, and now I was calling for money. I suddenly lost my nerve.

"No Mom," I answered. A white egret with a tall, curved neck and long black legs landed on the ground just beside me, and he stood staring at me with a small yellow eye that flitted to and fro.

"He tilled up the soil in the front yard, you know that ugly triangle of weeds that was there, tucked up against the fence under the plum tree?" I murmured something and she continued, "Well he got out there the other day while I was at the hair salon and tilled the soil up and lined up all these beautiful plants he'd purchased at the Merry Gardener store. He'd researched all the plants that would bloom throughout the year and could stand to be in the shade. I'm sure he had help from someone at the store because you know, dear, don't you, that your father has never been very good at that sort of thing..." she trailed off, and I could hear her swallowing her iced tea. "Anyway, I was out in the garden planting them and I got a little warm. The plants really are beautiful; they will fill the area in so nicely you know. In time for your next visit, I'm sure," she pressed.

"That's wonderful, Mom. Say, I'm sorry about your anniversary, I meant to call you and then I got busy and forgot," I lied. It was only a white lie though, I told myself, it was harmless and would make her feel better than finding out I had forgotten her anniversary altogether. I saw movement out of the corner of my eye and turned my head to find that the egret had taken several steps closer to me.

"No worries, dear, it's not your anniversary so I don't expect you to remember it," she said casually, and the guilt trip continued. "And how are you doing? Is work going okay?"

"It's going okay. I'm still working to get my commissions up," I decided to try the indirect approach. The whole "Life is so hard, I'm living off grilled cheese sandwiches and Gatorade" bit. It would elicit the compulsory offer to help out, to which I would feign refusal before finally giving in. "It's hard, you know, because you're trying to sell someone something they may have forgotten they ever wanted, and that makes it just like regular telemarketing calls. No one really likes those, but they're the bread and butter that make up my pay," I laid it on thick, preparing for the final drive. "And without them, I'm literally living on bread and butter." It was the money shot, the final blow to a nurturing mother's heart. Her youngest son, her baby boy, was living off nothing but bread and butter. I prepared myself for my Mom's offer of help and practiced my refusal in my head. Nothing too sincere, but something more of a non-specific word like "Nah..." would probably be perfect.

"Well sweetheart, what about the grocery money I've been sending? Is that not enough?"

This was not what I had been expecting. Had we already had this conversation and I had forgotten? I stopped doodling and sat up more erect, and the egret decided that was quite enough from someone he wasn't entirely sure of; he spread his wings and launched himself out over the water. A blue heron saw him and took flight as well, gliding low over the water as he searched for small prey fish.

"CJ? You still there?" my Mom asked.

"Yeah," I finally said, not knowing what else to say.

"I know, I know, you never wanted me to bring it up. I'm just concerned if it's enough. Believe me, dear, I'd send you more if I could figure out a way to hide it from your father," another pause and another sip of iced tea, "But it's been hard enough to hide away the little I have been sending. Honestly, I don't see what the big deal is, it's just food money for heaven's sake," her tone had become quieter, and I could picture her turning her head each way to make sure my Dad wasn't around to hear her.

"Sorry Mom, I don't know what you're talking about. You sure you got the right kid?" I suggested. Though it sounded bad, it was all too true, my Mom often confused us kids. My favorite bit while growing up was the name lottery, because it invariably destroyed what otherwise might have been a harsh reprimand. My name wasn't "Christopher", it was "Jackson-Trevor-Christopher," or perhaps when she was a little more flustered, impatient or pressed for time it became "Jack-Trev-Christopher," followed by a long pause as she tried to remember why she'd called to me in the first place. My brothers and I would snicker as we shuffled over to her, the three of us representing the conglomerate body that her name lottery had summoned. My Dad would sit in the corner, reading the newspaper and sighing.

"Quite sure. Marianne re-gifts back to us any money I tuck into cards and Julie – I honestly think she just shreds the checks. Whatever it is, she certainly doesn't deposit them. Wreaks total havoc on my checkbook balancing, but oh well. Those poor dears, too proud to accept the help, but I know they need it," my mother sighed. Marianne was Trevor's wife and Julie was Jackson's current girlfriend. I'd only met Marianne once, at the wedding, and I had never met Julie. If I ever did, I'd probably have a hard time getting to know her because of all the preconceived notions I had developed based on my mom's extensive descriptions.

"I don't remember asking you for any grocery money," I said honestly.

"Don't you? It was so sweet, too. I still have the card," Mom said, her voice echoing. Apparently she'd put me on speakerphone.

"I sent you a card asking for grocery money?" I asked incredulously, wracking my brain. I rarely sent cards out, and even less frequently did I write anything beyond "CJ" in them.

"It was the sweetest gesture. You know, I was so distraught over your leaving that I was driving your father crazy, and when I went into my purse for a tissue I found your card. It was so nice, you writing how you couldn't imagine what it would be like to live without my cooking every day, and you only hoped that one day you would meet a woman as attentive and caring," she sniffed, and I realized she was crying at the memory. The memory of a card I vaguely remembered leaving for her (did I really write something that mushy on it though? I wasn't entirely sure I had) but that I was fairly certain had nothing to do with a request for grocery money. "I almost didn't see the other part, you'd written it so small on the back, but when I flipped the card up to show your father, I spotted it."

"What did it say?" I asked, intrigued.

"You said that you knew it was a lot to ask, after all these years of support, and you were so embarrassed that you never wanted to mention it again, but you really felt certain that you would be struggling for grocery money for a while and wouldn't I please help just a little." Another sniff. "I never told your father, and when Travis gave me your PO Box, I just started sending the money orders." I could feel the hairs on the back of my neck stand up.

"Travis gave you a PO Box to send money to?"

"Well yes, dear. You never told me how much you needed and you weren't returning my calls, so I called Travis' phone to ask you. He told me how hard it was for you, finally out on your own but still not totally independent, and how hard you were trying. He said that you didn't even like to talk about it with him, because you found it to be too embarrassing. And believe me, I understand that. It can be so wonderfully freeing to move out on your own," another sniff, "But it's also so very hard. I don't think you ever quite realize what you actually need in order to make it by, but that's why I was so willing to help you. You should know that I'll always be willing to help—and I don't think ill of you needing any help, so you don't have to be embarrassed."

The blood rushed to my head and tingles crept down my spine. "How much have you sent, Mom?"

"You know, no matter how old you guys get, you're still my children, and I want to help you if you need it. At least you have a job and you're working hard, it would be different if you were just a lay about," she was justifying her actions the way she knew she would have to if my Dad ever found out that she was sending money to me. "I suppose I should've checked to see if you really needed it anymore, as I know that when you were promoted to supervisor you started to make more, but I figured you would tell me when you were all set and until then, I just couldn't bear the idea of cutting you off..."

"Mom," I said gently but firmly.

"Yes, honey?"

"How much have you sent?"

"Oh well let me see, now, I've sent two hundred dollars each month... well dear, I don't have a calculator..." her voice trailed off as she dug through drawers in search of a calculator. "Let's see, $200 a month for just around six years now..."

My mind raced, doing the math. $200 a month, twelve months a year for six years worked out to just over $14,000. I stood up, grabbing the notepad and turning back toward the office. I muttered some excuse to my Mom and ended the phone call, stepping into the office and making my way back to my desk. I placed the notepad down and began to collect my belongings, nearly jumping out of my skin when a hand came to rest on my shoulder.

"Leaving for the day?" a coworker, whose name I still failed to remember, asked. I nodded. He glanced down at my desk, spying my doodles. "Hey, the Marquesas Islands," he pointed at the notepad. I stared down to find the tell-tale horseshoe-shaped islands staring back at me. "You thinking of taking a trip down there? Great fishing!" He slapped me on the back and walked away.

***

Alamar stood at the helm, guiding the ship through the dangerous reefs and into the central lagoon. All was quiet on deck, leaving only the sound of the wind in the sails and the gentle lapping of the water against the ship. The water was shallow, too shallow to bring her in any closer, and Alamar finally raised his hand.

"Drop anchor," he ordered, letting his hand fall to emphasize the words. Five crew members moved in one motion, throwing the anchor into the water with a splash. "You," Alamar pointed at the slaves who were battered and beaten from six days' hard work without rest. "Make ready the treasure, we're going ashore." Duarte moved closer, leaning toward Alamar in confidence.

"The lagoon will protect the island from the weather well enough that we need not go too far inland. A hundred feet from the shore should be far enough." Alamar nodded.

"I'll go ashore with the slaves and bury the treasure," Alamar confided. It was too simple to be sincere, and Duarte shook his head.

"I cannot chart the map from here, you need me with you." Duarte feared his chances should he remain alone

onboard with the crew, and with the passing of time and increase of recovered treasure his distrust of Alamar had grown. Alamar smiled, a ghastly grin that revealed his half-rotten teeth.

"You won't chart the map from here," he confirmed. Duarte sighed in relief. "I will chart the map myself," Alamar continued, and Duarte sucked in his breath.

"But I —"

"You will remain on board," Alamar interrupted, his voice cold with finality. Duarte nodded, resolved to the fact that he had no choice in the matter. Alamar turned to the crew and raised his voice for all to hear, "And anyone who has a problem with that will answer to me, personally."

The slaves lowered the chests onto the skiff and it sank deeper into the water under the weight. The crew crowded the rail, watching intently as though they knew it may be the last time they would see the treasure. Duarte wondered how many of them feared for their lives as he did for his. He wondered how many of them were prepared to defend themselves against Alamar's greed.

Duarte watched Alamar's small skiff move away from the ship, the suspicion in his heart growing with every second that passed. He patted his shirt, feeling the bulk of the map within. It was now the most precious thing he held, and he guarded it closely. It was his key to the treasure. Actually, it was the only key to the treasure.

Once again I awoke to Sophie's cool hand on my forehead. The bright lights of the office shone down on me, and despite the cramped space there was still a sizable crowd gathered around me.

"What time is it?" I asked Sophie, pushing my way up despite the restraining arm she forced down on my shoulder.

"It's four-thirty in the afternoon," Sophie said. "You should just relax, there's an ambulance on its way and I think you should get checked out." I shook my head.

"I'm fine, I don't need an ambulance," I said, pushing harder to get to my feet.

"CJ, you passed out while standing up, falling straight backwards. If nothing else you probably have a concussion," Sophie's voice was urgent, and she sounded more than concerned. She sounded scared.

"Really, I'm fine," I answered. "I need to go," I struggled to move through the crowd to my desk, grabbing up my few things and shoving them into my pockets.

"CJ!" Sophie's voice was loud and authoritative. "You really should just take it easy for a moment." I smiled, trying to calm her nerves.

"I'm fine," I said calmly, encouragingly. "I just need to get home. Trust me, it's okay," I added. I saw her face soften, but only a little.

"Are you sure?" she asked.

"I'm sure. It's nothing to be worried about," I lied. It <u>was</u> something to be worried about; I understood that now.

"Would you like a ride home?" Sophie asked. I smiled again.

"No thanks, the bus will be just fine," I said. I pushed my chair under the table and moved off, dispersing the crowd of coworkers who had gathered to see what was happening.

As I stood at the bus stop waiting, I stopped resisting and let my mind drift over what had just happened. All this time I thought I was suffering from vivid nightmares, but now I understood that this was not what they were. They were too familiar, too concise, and too detailed. They weren't dreams at all—they were flashbacks, and I had little time left to resolve their cause.

Chapter 21

I stepped off the bus, so self-involved that I stumbled over the last step. Luckily I was able to prevent a face plant by some fancy footwork that I'm sure would've impressed even Michael Flatley. I hardly noticed the cloud of brown exhaust that shrouded me as the bus moved away from the stop; I was focused instead on the endless line of cars that prevented me from crossing the street. It appeared that so many vehicles were moving up and down the street that it would never be entirely clear; I was looking for just enough of a break that I could bolt across safely. I found it hard to concentrate, twice stepping into the road and being forced back to the safety of the sidewalk by angry horns. Apparently I wasn't the only one in a hurry.

Finally, a traffic light stopped the cars approaching from my left and an elderly woman in a Cadillac dramatically slowed the cars approaching from my right. While those who were stuck behind her honked their horns and cursed, I was only too grateful as I jogged across the street through the gap.

As soon as I turned onto our street, I noticed something had changed. It didn't take a Sherlock Holmes to figure out that the Lincoln Town car that had been parked several doors down from our house for most of the last week had moved from its spot. It now sat almost directly in front of our house, its rear bumper just barely edging over the line into our neighbor's driveway. I was hardly surprised to discover that their surveillance was of someone more closely related to me than my neighbor, but still I felt nervousness flutter in my stomach. I knew it would be worse if I tried to turn and walk away, so I kept my pace steady as I walked up the driveway and onto the front porch. Out of the corner of my eye I noticed the passenger-side door of the Lincoln open, and a leg thrust out onto the ground. I shoved my key into the lock and turned it, pushing open the door.

"Travis?" I called out as I stepped into the house and swung the door closed behind me. I figured I had about ten seconds to collect myself before our visitors would be at the door. I used the time wisely, quickly making my way through the rooms to confirm that there was no one home. As I came to Travis' room I paused in shock. It looked like the aftermath of a hurricane, clothes and coat hangers strewn about the floor, sheets pulled off the mattress and the mattress half-off the box spring, books lying open and face-down around the floor. The disarray was so distinctive that I thought maybe we'd been robbed, and I turned to check my room when I spotted something. It was a bit of paper wedged in between the mattress and box-spring, now partially exposed since the two no longer sat flush together. I leaned over and picked it up, unfolding the paper to reveal a hand-drawn map. I stared down at the familiar shapes outlined in pencil, and was surprised by the sudden, sharp rap on the front door. I hurriedly re-folded the map and shoved it into my pocket, turning back to the front of the house. I managed a glimpse at my room as I passed it in the hall, and noticed that everything looked normal.

"Good afternoon," I was greeted as soon as I opened the door. The man before me was tall and wiry, with thinning brown hair, black rim glasses and a real bummer of an overbite. He had his hand on the door frame, and while he wasn't leaning on it he still had the air of an individual who was completely at ease. The man beside him was shorter, heavier, and obviously the obligatory muscle. He had thick, bushy eyebrows that hid small, dark eyes, and I was quite certain that he rarely smiled.

"Nice house," Thin mentioned casually, rapping his knuckles on the door frame. "Mind if we come in?" he asked, nosily pushing his face forward to glance around the living room. Eyebrows just stared forward, unmoving.

"Mind if I ask who you are?" I returned with more gumption than I thought I had in me. My heart was pounding so hard that I was sure they could both hear it.

"That would be a bit pointless," Thin replied, "We're here to talk with your friend, Travis," Thin called back over his shoulder.

"He's not home right now," I answered. "Who would you say you were with?" I tried again. I was no longer certain that my own guess was correct, and I suddenly felt very uncomfortable about the idea of being alone with these two individuals inside a closed space. Where no one could see us. Or hear us. Or...

"I wouldn't," Thin said, cutting through my thoughts. "When's the last time you saw Mr. Graven?"

"You know, I'm really not in the habit of discussing personal details with strangers. If you don't mind, I have some work to do, so ..." I began to swing the door shut, only to find that it wouldn't budge. I hadn't seen the movement, but Eyebrows had his arm pressed firmly against the door, holding it open. The moment my eyes fell on his arm, he moved it and stood back, crossing his arms across his chest. This only served to accentuate how thick his upper arms were, and I made a mental note not to tick him off. Thin moved forward.

"It would be in your best interest to let us in and answer our questions, Mr. Durbrin," Thin brought his face uncomfortably close to mine. I glanced up, noticing hair plugs not so cleverly hidden on a dry scalp.

The map was burning a hole in my pocket and I ached to get another look at it, but I had to admit that Thin was probably right. I had seriously considered calling the cops, once I gathered my wits enough to sort out my story, but they were unlikely to have the resources that a government agency, like the one I wanted to believe these guys were with, would have. If I talked to them, they were less likely to charge me as an accessory (I hoped) and more likely to help me (I hoped). I sighed and stepped back, allowing the door to swing further into the house. Thin moved forward, treading lightly on his toes and the balls of his feet. Eyebrows followed, his steps firm and heavy. Once inside, he shut the door behind him and again crossed his arms to stand still and quiet. Thin had apparently accepted my invitation to come in as extending to a full inspection of the house, and he walked slowly around, glancing down the hallway and in through open doors. He nodded toward Travis' disheveled belongings.

"How long has he been gone?" he asked, running his eyes over the mess and blinking. I wondered if he had a photographic memory and was recording everything he saw.

"I don't know that he is gone," I answered. "He had already left the house when I went to work this morning, and he's not here now, but that's not particularly unusual," I added. *Stealing fourteen thousand dollars from my parents is, though,* I said quietly to myself. It was beyond me why I still felt an impulse to protect him, despite everything I knew that he had done, and despite knowing that there were likely far worse things he had done that I still didn't know about. Hell, the presence of two government agents in our house seemed to confirm that last point. But perhaps that was exactly why – because no matter what had been done, no one ever felt totally comfortable being entirely truthful with government agencies. They weren't exactly applauded for their friendly attitudes and helpful nature, and were probably guilty of more crimes committed under the guise of "duty" than eighty percent of the population. And what the hell gave them the right to know all of your deepest, darkest secrets without revealing any of their own? *Screw them all,* I turned angry eyes on Thin, who met my gaze with his own cold stare. I dropped my eyes to the floor.

"So last night is the last time you saw him?" Thin pressed.

"Look, I figure you probably know more than I do or you wouldn't be here. It's hard to believe that after staking out the house for a month, you lost him," I trailed off, watching Thin's face. He glanced at Eyebrows, and while Eyebrows' face showed nothing, Thin's betrayed a subtle emotion that was not meant for me to see. I did anyway, and I asked incredulously, "You lost him?"

"Mr. Graven managed to … elude us while we were following him yesterday. At the Tampa Airport he purchased several tickets to multiple destinations. Due to an unfortunate – mix-up, we lost him through the security checkpoint."

I shrugged. Obviously these guys had to be some small time, local detectives. There was no way that Federal agents, with the resources they had at their disposal, could have lost Travis through something as minor as an airport security checkpoint. Once again, I surprised myself with a feeling of relief, knowing that Travis was still okay. What was that? It was immediately followed by another thought—if these guys were small time detectives, who had hired them?

"Look, I realize you guys have a bit of a problem on your hands, but I really don't think I have any information that will help you." Of course I was lying my pants off, but I was no longer certain they could do anything for me and I was beginning to feel impatient.

Thin turned to Eyebrows, who nodded. It suddenly occurred to me that the silent one was the senior one—the one in control. Thin moved toward the sofa, indicating with his hand.

"Mind if we sit?" I shook my head and he sat down, pulling his suit jacket out from under him and crossing his right leg over his left knee. Eyebrows remained standing, though he had moved closer to us and uncrossed his arms. I moved over to the armchair and sat down, facing the two of them.

"There's something you need to know about the man you know as Travis Graven," Thin began. I swallowed my tongue.

"The man I know as?" I questioned. "What do you mean the man I know as?"

"I mean that this is not his legal name. He was born Colten Turney, and he has used a handful of aliases over the years. Travis Graven is his safe name – the one he's never used while working a job," Thin explained, pulling a cigarette from his pocket and placing it in between his lips. As he flicked a lighter open he paused and glanced up at me. "Do you mind?" he asked. I shook my head, too stunned to comprehend the question. He lit the cigarette and inhaled deeply.

"Jobs?" I finally asked. I felt as though I was a small child wading through three feet of snow. My thoughts were sluggish and slow, and I no longer knew what was worse—not knowing what Travis had been up to or finally finding out that everything I had imagined was real, and then some.

"Turney is a con man. His success is probably largely due to his versatility—he never pulls the same con for longer than three months, and he completely changes his appearance between each job. He has a charming personality that, while it can be warm, is deceptively flawed as well. It makes him real, vulnerable, and believable," another draw, another puff of white smoke.

"I'm sorry, but I find this hard to believe," I began. Inside my head a voice asserted, *No, you don't.* "I mean, I'm not here to defend Travis as being the most honorable character in the world—having been his roommate for awhile now I know better than most that he has plenty of flaws all his own. But he had a rough beginning in life, and while that doesn't justify some of the things he's done," I thought about the house and my mother's money, "I think I know him well enough to say that he's a good guy who just sometimes goes a little astray." Once again I was defending him, and I just didn't understand why. Deep down I knew, I had always known, that something about Travis was off. I had always felt that there was some ulterior motive for his befriending me, like he was setting me up for something. But at the same time, I just could never bring myself to back away. I felt scared–like if I didn't befriend and defend him, I would suddenly see through all his facades and realize who he truly was. And that was something I absolutely wasn't ready for.

Thin reached his hand up, snapping his fingers in the air. Eyebrows stepped forward, pulling a file out of his expansive inner coat pocket and placing it in Thin's hand. The cigarette had been forgotten, and it was slowly burning its way closer to Thin's fingers, the ash growing precariously long. Thin flipped the file open, pulling out a photograph and shoving it at me. It showed an apparently happy family; mother, father, two boys and three girls sitting before a Christmas tree. I'd never seen a photograph of Travis when he was younger, but the chubby smiling face of one of the boys was undoubtedly his.

"Colten Turney was born into a wealthy family. His father was a top executive at a snack food plant and his mother inherited a healthy sum from her parents when they passed on. He was born and raised in Santa Clarita– in fact you two attended the same school for awhile when you were around eight years old," Thin paused and turned to Eyebrows, who nodded. I choked out what might've been a gasp.

"Colt? Travis is...Colt?" my mind raced and whirled, I sank back against the couch, my heart pounding.

"Yes, he went by Colt at the time. He was given everything a kid could ask for, he was rarely disciplined, and he had an excellent tutor. When he was eight years old he started having nightmares, and they seemed to affect his behavior and personality so intensely that his parents had him see a therapist. After a few sessions with the therapist, he returned home and made a request for something he wanted," Thin's lips twitched for a moment, as though he were trying to suppress a sneeze, and then he continued. "His parents denied him for the first time in his life, and three years later he ran away from home and was never heard from again. It was like something inside of him suddenly snapped, and he became someone else entirely," Thin handed me another photograph, this time of a sullen kid who stared back at the camera as though he wanted to strangle it. "Colten managed to get into the foster care system for awhile, though it's not entirely clear how he managed to disconnect himself from the kid that was the object of an impressive, nationwide manhunt. He bounced around from foster home to foster home for five years, and then disappeared from there too. Since then, he has pulled a variety of cons across the country, from selling bogus water filtration systems to emptying bank accounts under false pretenses," another draw on the cigarette, and the ash grew even longer and more fragile. "Just as things start to heat up, he disappears."

"What was it?" I asked. Thin frowned at me. "What did he want that his parents denied?" I saw something cross Eyebrows' face – what might have been a smile if he hadn't suppressed it with a grimace. Thin gave in, letting the smile extend from ear to ear. It was a hideous grin, and terribly ironic under the circumstances.

"He told his parents he wanted his pirate ship back, and he wouldn't accept it without its treasure," Thin shoved the cigarette in through the grin, closing his lips and drawing deeply before releasing the cigarette. Eyebrows grimaced harder and I had the feeling it was his way of laughing.

I shook my head in disbelief, even as the jigsaw pieces began to fit together in my mind. As I opened my mouth to ask another question, Thin interrupted me.

"The one thing we can't figure out is his latest venture," Thin lifted the cigarette, inspecting it closely as he turned it in between his fingers. The long finger of ash fell onto the carpet and he slid his foot over it, suffocating out any possible embers.

"What's that?" I asked on cue, slightly disgusted by the ash now pressed into the carpet.

"You," Thin said cryptically, standing and moving to the door. He pulled the door open, flicking the cigarette out into the front yard before closing the door and moving back to the sofa.

"Me?" I asked, once again aware of the map in my pocket.

"You. Turney has never remained close to anyone for very long. He certainly has never kept a safe house in one location for more than six months at a time. Yet he stayed with you in Santa Clarita for over six years. He even went straight for a while, disappearing for a few years before he started pulling jobs again. He persisted in returning back to Santa Clarita time and again. Clearly there is something in this relationship for him. Something big enough to risk being caught for. Can you figure what that might be, Mr. Durbrin?" Thin leaned in closer, and even Eyebrows took a step further into the living room.

I could feel sweat beginning to form on my back. My heart was pounding so hard I could barely breathe, but I shook my head.

"Do you know why Turney would want to go to," Thin pulled a small sheet of paper from his inner coat pocket and unfolded it, "Paris, Hawaii, Miami, Amsterdam or Greece?" He replaced the paper in his pocket and stared at me for a few more moments. "We cannot protect you if you don't tell us what he wants from you."

"I'm still trying to grasp what you're telling me," I answered truthfully, shaking my head in disbelief. "I have no idea why anyone like that would want to hang around me," I lied—the virtual fire burning through my pocket becoming unbearable.

Thin's eyes searched my face. He either decided that I was a terrible liar, or that I was innocent but in total shock, and he stood.

"Let us know if you change your mind, Mr. Durbrin," he said over his shoulder. I remained seated, not trusting my legs to hold my weight. Eyebrows remained a moment longer, staring at me as though to imprint me with a message. I understood that he was not a man to be trifled with.

As the engine of the Lincoln started and then became faint, I finally trusted myself to move. I stood and walked into the bathroom, closing the door and locking it before flipping on the switches for the light and the fan. Certain that there was no way I could be seen or overheard, I pulled the map out of my pocket and carefully unfolded it onto the counter. A small puddle soaked through the center of the map and I swore, picking the map up and wiping the counter with a dry washcloth. As I sat the map back down I felt the familiar sensation of déjà vu.

The map had been hand-drawn, probably by Travis himself, and showed a group of small islands. At the top of the map Travis had written "Mule Keys", and on the right side an arrow pointing east with "Key West" written just above it. The islands had been named, Boca Grande Key being the westernmost and clearly the largest. Large red x's had been drawn over all of the islands, except Boca Grande Key, which was circled several times and accentuated with a series of question marks.

I continued to stare at the map for another ten minutes, the elusive final jigsaw piece starting to outline in my mind.

"I need a map," I said aloud as I refolded and pocketed Travis' map and unlocked the bathroom door. There was no way Travis had flown to Paris, Hawaii, Amsterdam or Greece. My hunch was that he was in Key West.

***

The hurricane struck suddenly, wind battering the sails and angry black waves slamming the sides of the ship, as though it were determined to tear her to shreds. The crew and slaves looked like rag dolls, rolled and tossed around the deck. Each time a wave washed over the deck Duarte was certain it would be the last, the ship keeling dangerously to the side and threatening to capsize. He clung desperately to the mast, tired, cold and wet and wondering just how much longer he could stand it.

They had left the calmer waters to the north, moving back toward a route home, but the hurricane had forced them to the north again, and once again they were in danger of running aground on the reefs and sandbars. The rigging creaked and moaned under the forceful hand of the whipping wind. Duarte's stomach flip-flopped and his heart raced.

Alamar's face appeared suddenly, inches in front of Duarte's. He stood unsteadily on the deck, rocking with the ship and somehow managing to keep to his feet with great effort. His eyes carried a look of desperation.

"Give me the map!" he shouted above the storm. Duarte gritted his teeth, tightening his grip on the mast as another wave slammed into the ship. Alamar's face came even closer. "The map, Duarte!" he demanded. Duarte shook his head, flinging water from his hair.

"It's not yours, Alamar," Duarte found his voice, weak but certain. "It's of equal share for all of us," he absently patted his shirt, unintentionally revealing the map's location. Alamar's face lit up, his smile frightening Duarte into releasing his hold on the mast to better defend himself. Alamar's strong hand gripped Duarte's shirt, holding him firmly in place. The map appeared suddenly in Alamar's hand, disappearing just as quickly into his own shirt before he turned, dragging Duarte with him.

"Not anymore," Alamar breathed into Duarte's ear. As another wave forced the ship to keel hard to port, Alamar released his hold and Duarte slid across the sloped deck, smacking his head against the rail before toppling overboard into the dark, angry sea.

I sat up on the floor, rubbing the sweat from my forehead. I glanced at the map book on the coffee table that had been thrown open to a page entitled "The Florida Keys". I traced my finger along the key islands, pausing at Key West before moving further down to the Mule Keys. I pulled Travis' map out and compared the two, they were near identical and from the looks of it, Travis' map had been traced over the map in the book. As I sat up, my eyes drifted to the left, falling on a small set of islands further west. They were familiar shapes that I knew well, even though I could swear I'd never seen them before. They formed a lopsided circle of disconnected islands, and bore the name "Marquesas Keys". Déjà vu blurred my vision as the last jigsaw piece fell into place in my mind.

Chapter 22

It's hard to say where courage comes from, but in my case it was the result of living in fear and cowardice for far too long and feeling the powerful urge to finally face my own personal Goliath.

Though my mind still reeled with the spiritual ramifications, I had mostly come to terms with the fact that I had long experienced flashbacks to an earlier life. This acceptance opened the door to memories that were both distant and familiar, not the least of which was the memory of an unresolved conflict which had begun long ago, and was now approaching its climax.

In my determination to achieve my goal, I wove a story convincing enough to get a hefty loan from my father, and within twenty-four hours of my encounter with Thin and Eyebrows I was sitting in a terminal at the Tampa International Airport, waiting for my flight to Key West. In my pocket was the hand-drawn map I had found between Travis' mattresses, untouched except for a small notation I had made on the map, just west of Boca Grande Key in the Mule Keys group.

Finally, after an hour spent impatiently waiting, an airline attendant approached the podium and called my flight. She then moved over to stand in front of an open door, directing the nineteen passengers on the flight through a gate that dumped us outdoors onto a small, covered walkway. I shouldered my backpack and followed the other passengers down the walkway to a Beechcraft 1900, the small "puddle-jumper" aircraft that would fly us 240 miles south to the island of Key West. I purposely stood at the rear of the small line, prolonging my time before I would have to stuff myself into the tiny plane, like one more sardine in a crowded tin can. When it was my turn, I climbed up the short flight of stairs and hunched over to fit into the aircraft. Luckily my assigned seat was near the front so I didn't have far to go. I fell into my seat, shoving my backpack under the seat in front of me and fastening my seat belt. The pre-flight announcements whizzed by and it wasn't long before we were taxiing the runway, sandwiched in by the bigger jets around us. As our turn came the engines revved to full speed and I fought the urge to shove my fists into my ears to drown out the noise. A pair of headphones peeked from the seat pocket in front of me and I grabbed them, gently but firmly settling them over my ears. They weren't the best at noise-cancellation, but it was better than nothing so I left them in place, plugging them into my armrest and finding a rock station.

A traveler's guide that had been shoved into the seat pocket in front of me was now partially hanging out of it, and I pulled it to my lap. On the front was a large advertisement for the Key West Shipwreck HISTOREUM® Museum, which was devoted to displaying the story and artifacts of the wrecked *Isaac Allerton,* a sea vessel that sank off the Keys in 1856. I grinned and pushed the guide back into the pocket, closing my eyes and leaning back in my seat.

The trip took an hour and ten minutes; it felt like we had hardly reached our cruising altitude before we began our descent. I peered out the window and saw the beautiful blue waters of the Gulf, with hints of paler greens and blues where the water was shallow. The Key islands stretched out behind and in front of the plane, connected by the thin line of the Overseas Highway. To the west was the seemingly endless stretch of the Gulf of Mexico, the sun catching the water and throwing bright reflections back at me.

The pilot set the Beechcraft gently down on the single runway that comprised the Key West airport, and taxied to the terminal. Once again we were escorted off the plane and onto the tarmac, walking a short distance into the terminal. My fellow passengers headed for the baggage claim, while I shouldered my backpack and headed for the exit. As I once again stepped outside into the sunshine I glanced around for a taxi stand and found it set up to my right. I approached the stand and a man who was at least three inches taller than me, and very likely fifty pounds heavier, stood up and greeted me with a wide smile.

"Need a taxi?" he asked in a southern drawl that would've been right at home in Atlanta. I nodded. "Whereya headed?" he asked as he whistled and motioned to someplace behind me.

"The Dry Tortugas ferry," I answered as the cab pulled up to the curb.

"Grinnell Street ferry terminal," the man called in to the cabbie as he held the back door open for me. I slid into the car, pushing my backpack along the seat next to me. Before I'd managed to get in far enough to shut the door behind me, the cabbie hit the gas, pushing me back against the seat and forcing the door to shut on its own. I impulsively reached for the seat belt, grabbing at thin air.

"There's no belts in the back," the cabbie said, eyeing me from his rear-view mirror. I nodded, wrapping my hand around the door handle and gripping until my knuckles turned white. A few moments later the cabbie jerked a fist to the left, shouting over his shoulder, "Further down that way is Smather's Beach. The southernmost point in the US, though actually there's a tip off the fort that's a bit further. You're now closer to Havana, Cuba than you are to Miami." He spat out the window just as a car passed. That was going to be a nice little surprise for the driver the next time he grabbed the door handle.

White Street, about one and a half miles long, brought us from the southern side of the island directly across to the northwestern side. A few minutes later the driver stopped, turning to collect his fare. I glanced up to the dash, looking for the meter that wasn't there. As I opened my mouth to ask the cabbie about his missing meter, my eyes fell on a white sticker affixed to the back of the driver's seat.

Airport Fares
$10.00 flat – Anywhere in Key West

I supposed that was fair – it had only been about four miles and fifteen minutes, but anything less than ten dollars probably wasn't worth it, considering gas prices alone. I pulled my money from my pocket, unfolded a ten and a couple ones (I assumed you still tipped on a flat fare), and placed the money in the cabbie's hand. Once again I had hardly stepped out of the cab, the door still open against my hand, when he sped off, the door slamming shut on its own. I shook my head – the guy belonged in New York City, not a laid-back island town like Key West. I walked to the ocean front and then headed along the walkway in a southwestern direction, away from the ferry terminal and toward the marina.

The marina at Key West's Historic Seaport was not unlike those I had seen in Tarpon Springs. There were several signs for boat rentals, but as I made my way up to each stand I was informed that there were no more rentals available for the next few days. I was about to give up when I saw a man sitting in a beach chair under a wide umbrella. He had gray hair that was long and messy, tangled by the ever-present breeze. His face and head were lobster red, but I guessed that was probably normal for Key West. To one side of the man was a cooler with a can of beer and a small radio perched on top, and to the other was a small dog, looking more dead than asleep. In front of the man was a barely legible sign that advertised boat rentals. His eyes fixed on me as I approached, and he leaned forward while remaining in his chair.

"You lookin' for a boat?" Red asked when I was five feet away. At the sound of his voice the dog sat up suddenly, and I was relieved to discover that he was alive after all.

"Yeah, do you have anything available for tomorrow?" I asked, shrugging as though it wasn't that important. If he did have anything left and he knew he was the only one he might try and gouge me on the rental. If I acted like I didn't care one way or the other, the gouging may not be as bad. At least, that's what I hoped.

"I've got a sixteen-foot skiff that's available t'morrow. You looking for all day or haf day?" Red asked. The dog decided there was nothing interesting to be up for, and flopped back over onto his side.

"All day," I answered. "I want to get out and see some of the smaller islands," I said nondescriptly.

"Which ones?" Red asked as he grabbed his beer and chugged the remaining half of the can before crumpling it in his hands and setting it on the ground.

"Just the local ones here – the Mule Keys. I understand the Dry Tortugas are a bit farther out."

"Not too bad – a couple hours each way. The skiff has ninety horsepower, it'll get you out there and back in a day if you really wanna go," Red held up the radio with one hand while opening the cooler and grabbing another beer with the other. A piece of ice dropped to the ground and the dog suddenly jumped up, swallowed the ice, and flopped back down.

"Nah, don't want to go out that far," I said.

"Well you know you can't go ashore on the Mule Keys – can't hardly anchor off many of them either. Except the northwest side of Boca Grande. If you go out to the Dry Tortugas you can walk around Fort Jefferson." Another long chug on the beer can. "Of course, if you do wanna go out there I'd recommend the ferry. It's cheaper than renting a boat, and comes with some nice amenities." A large belch rounded out the sentence, sending beer fumes my way. I held back the compulsory gag, turning and pulling a deep breath of fresh air into my lungs.

"What's it cost to rent the skiff?" I asked once I'd composed myself.

"It's two-hundred and ninety-five dollars for the day. Now that's from seven o'clock in the morning until six o'clock in the afternoon."

"That's a bit steep," I commented, having no frame of reference to truly judge by.

"Well sonny, that's the price. I ain't here to cut no bargain discounts. Gotta feed the family you know," another chug of beer.

"I understand," I shrugged, turning to walk away and hoping he stopped me. I heard his chair creak and smiled.

"Hey there," Red said. I turned casually, "What?" written plainly across my face. Red extended his arm out, waving it into the marina. "If you want to save some money there's a young fella, about your age, going out to the Mule Keys t'morrow. Pr'ally would give you a lift for a fraction of the cost of renting your own boat." My blood turned cold, the smile erased from my face.

"What's he look like?"

"Well I dunno. Can't be much older than you, a little shorter maybe and pretty well-fed. Seems pretty nice, says he's out doing some marine research. He's been here off-and-on for a while now, really seems to know what he's doing. He said he has a government pass to land around the Mule Keys for his research, so maybe you'd get lucky and be able to go ashore after all," another chug of beer. "You okay?" he asked, a concerned look on his face. I realized I was standing with my mouth hanging open, so I closed it and nodded.

"Yeah, I'm fine. Thanks for the tip!" I turned and walked away, failing to notice when Red shouted after me one final time.

Chapter 23

The next morning I woke up a half hour before my requested wake-up call at five-thirty a.m. I dressed quickly, skipping a shower and running my fingers through my hair in an attempt to straighten it out and flatten it down. I pulled on a light cotton t-shirt and khaki shorts, stepping into a pair of sandals before pushing my toiletries and dirty clothes into my backpack and practically running out the door. I stopped in the lobby of the motel for two minutes to drop off my keys and grab a bagel before heading out to the marina.

At six a.m. I sat across the street from the marina, hiding behind the trunk of a palm tree and eyeing a small blue motorboat that sat at the dock. Red had pointed the boat out to me, and I was sure the young man he'd rented it to was Travis. Now I just had to wait for him to show. I wasn't quite ready for Travis to know I was here, so I had returned to Red yesterday afternoon, shelled out three hundred dollars for the skiff rental, plus another two hundred for a security deposit, and I was now prepared to follow Travis out to Boca Grande. Red had made it perfectly clear that no one left before seven a.m., but I wanted to be early just in case Travis decided to bend the rules.

A long forty-five minutes passed, and the adrenaline of excitement began to wear off. I began to second-guess every decision I had made in the last day, week, months, years… The truth was that there were no guarantees that Red had rented his boat to Travis. In fact, there were no guarantees that Travis was even here in Key West. I stood up to stretch my legs, and considered walking down to the corner store for a snack. Just as I turned, Travis appeared. Or at least, someone who walked like Travis appeared. He looked a bit taller (lifts?) and had blonde hair tucked under a sports cap (dyed?). His skin looked darker than normal (spray-on tan?) but he still had the confident stride I had come to know well over the last seven years. I couldn't believe the changes that had occurred in the last four days, and I marveled over Travis' ability to transform his appearance so that he truly looked like someone else.

Travis approached Red with a comfortable smile, and I knew he was sweet-talking his way into getting the boat a few minutes early. Red's somber countenance broke out into a smile, and he leaned forward with his hand outstretched, placing keys into Travis' hand. Travis gave Red another winning smile and strode down the dock to the boat. A few moments later he was slowly motoring out of the marina toward the Gulf waters. I forced myself to remain behind the palm tree a little longer before striding across the street and up to Red.

"Hey, you just missed your guy," Red said as I approached, throwing a thumb over his shoulder. "He's a really nice kid and I still think he could've saved you a pretty penny," he reached down and thumbed open what I hoped was his first beer of the day.

"Yeah – that's all right," I said casually, holding my hand out expectantly. Red didn't move. "So the skiff – it's ready to go?" I pressed. Red smiled and shook his head.

"Ain't seven o'clock yet," he said as he slurped his beer. I glanced down at my phone, pressing a button to illuminate the clock.

"It's six fifty-eight," I said, showing him my phone. He shook his head.

"Just hold yer horses, sonny," he threw the can back a little harder, missing his mouth and splashing some beer onto his dog. The dog didn't move.

"But you let Tr – er, the other guy go early," I pointed out. Red smiled again.

"And for another hundred I'll let you go early too," more beer. I shook my head.

As I waited for the next two minutes to pass by I wondered how hard it would be to follow Travis without being spotted. There was no need to race after him, I was pretty sure he was headed to Boca Grande anyway. Still, it would be nice to keep him in my sights at all times. Especially since he...Red stood up suddenly, interrupting my thoughts.

"*Now* it's seven o'clock," he pulled a small ring of keys from his pocket and held them out to me. "Bring 'er back by six p.m. or you'll have to pay another day," he warned, shaking a long, skinny finger at me. I nodded.

"Thanks," I took the keys and pushed them into my pocket. I strode quickly down the dock to the skiff that was tied to the end, stepping into the vessel before unwinding the cord and pushing off. I turned the keys in the ignition and the motor started smoothly, purring as I slowly made my way out into the warm blue waters of the Gulf.

Despite the early hour, the Gulf waters were already clogged with boat traffic. It was easy to spot Travis' blue boat; it was the only one holding a straight course to the west. The others boats seemed to be lazily drifting around, no specific destination in mind. The boat occupants were either lounging in the sun or staring down into the clear, blue water, sometimes pointing excitedly as some sea creature glided by. I carefully made my way around an assortment of luxury yachts and various sailboats and out into the open gulf.

As I crossed the Northwest Channel, the small Mule Key islands dotted the horizon, blocking my ability to clearly spot Travis' boat. I slowed the skiff and pulled my backpack onto my lap, unzipping the front pocket and removing Travis' hand drawn map. I pulled the skiff to the south toward the waters of the Atlantic, eventually passing Mule Key and making my way toward Crawfish Key, Man Key, Ballast Key, Woman Key, and finally Boca Grande.

Red had said that anchoring off Boca Grande was only permitted on the northwestern side of the small island, so I circled the island to the left, keeping a lookout for Travis' boat. As I neared the approved anchoring site I noticed two small vessels anchored offshore, neither of them the small blue motorboat Travis had left the marina in. My heart sank as I realized that he must have gone to one of the other islands, and there was no way for me to know which one. I glanced down at his map, but found nothing that would indicate what would draw him anyplace else. The other islands were clearly crossed off, and Boca Grande Key was circled boldly several times. As I scanned the map more closely, a small red mark became apparent. It was subtle, almost as if it had been placed there entirely by accident, and just on the northeastern side of Boca Grande Key. I decided that Travis must have gone there. I imagined it couldn't be far to walk from where I was, the entire island was only about eight hundred thousand square meters. On the other hand, the island was also flooded with water lagoons deeper inland, so I would have to stick to the mangroves closest to the strip of beach that bordered the entire northern half of the island.

I drifted the skiff closer to the other anchored vessels and shut off the motor, dropping the small anchor into the water. Pulling my backpack up onto my shoulders, I stepped off the skiff and into the shallow water, making my way up to the small, white beach laid out before me. The beach was deserted, and I assumed the owners of the other vessels were inland, exploring. I stood for a moment and listened to the quiet sounds of the island, the gentle waves pushing against the sand as it deposited small shells on the beach and the wind blowing gently through the mangrove bushes, whispering secrets no one would ever decipher.

The most direct way to get to the northeastern side of the island would be to stick to the beach, but I was loathe to remain that visible in case Travis *was* here. It looked like a couple small trails had been carved through the mangroves; I followed one that looked like it was leading east. I pushed my way along the narrow trail, feeling the beads of sweat begin to trickle down my back as the temperature slowly rose and the gulf breeze slowly disappeared. The trail dumped me onto another part of the white beach and my breath caught in my throat. Travis' blue boat was anchored only a few hundred feet southeast of the shore. I immediately felt vulnerable, and I stepped backwards into the mangroves, dropping my backpack to the ground. No sooner did it fall than a strong arm crossed my chest and the cool steel of a sharp blade pressed against my throat.

"Hello CJ," Travis' voice oozed. I moved to face him but his grip was strong, and he pressed the blade harder against my throat. I relaxed, letting out my breath.

"Hello Travis. Or is it Colten? Colten Turney?" I asked. The sweat on my back turned cold, despite the heat, and I suppressed a convulsive shiver. *I won't give in to fear*, I told myself.

"You know, I always hated that name. My parents made it worse by naming my siblings much more simply – Brandon, Susan, Robin and Jessica. It was like they wanted to force me to be different," his voice betrayed a deep pain I'd never heard from him before, and the knife moved away from my throat.

"Who *are* you?" I said slowly, and then in a fast motion dropped down and away from him, spinning to face him. An eerie smile curved the right side of his mouth.

"I won't insult either of us by answering that," Travis held the knife out toward me, the blade glinting in the sun. "We go way back, you and I. We've been here before," he waved his free arm around. My adrenaline started pumping faster and I shook my head in denial.

"You've lied to me–I don't even know how many times," my voice broke with raw emotion.

"Oh, did I hurt your feelings?" Travis mocked, tugging at his goatee. His coldness erased my lingering feelings of fear and betrayal, replacing them with hot anger. I slid my right foot slowly through the sand, hoping to catch it on a rock or large shell.

"You betrayed my trust," I answered as my foot caught on something hard. I used my heel to dislodge it from the sand, feeling for its size.

"Sometimes it has to be broken, before it can know true strength," Travis rationalized. "After all, how can you determine the strength of anything until you've driven it to its breaking point at least once?"

"You're a thief," I accused, digging harder with my heel.

"Well that's all in the way you look at it," Travis continued to point the knife at me, but he had relaxed into making broad gesticulations. "I prefer to think that I'm educating those who are stupid enough to be taken in. And if they fail to be educated, they deserve to be separated from their valuables."

"You're a murderer," I threw out, finding that my apparent weapon now wiggled freely.

"Now that's not really true," Travis frowned. "We both slipped, you just fell harder and further."

"This is madness," I stated flatly, glancing down at my foot to identify the object I'd uncovered.

"Genius is borne of madness," Travis sneered. My breath caught in my throat, forming a strangled gasp as my eyes rose to meet his.

"Alamar," I choked out involuntarily, my voice a whisper in my throat.

"See now, I knew you remembered me," he moved closer to me, the point of the knife only inches from my throat.

"How did you..."

"Find you? With great difficulty," he took another step closer, forcing me backwards onto the beach. "Remember when we first met? In elementary school? I didn't understand what was happening to me–I thought I was going crazy. I tried to tell myself that I was just having nightmares. Every kid has nightmares right?" he asked quizzically, rhetorically. "When they became violently persistent my parents took me to a sleep therapist," he scowled, the words dripping out of his mouth. "Some therapist he was. All he did was drug me up on fifteen different meds. They practically killed me, the bastards," he spat the word venomously, spittle shooting from his mouth. "But the dreams persisted, eventually coming at all times of the day and night. I finally realized what they really were, and stopped taking the meds in order to better remember. My parents couldn't handle it, and they tried to force the meds on me. They kept telling me I was unwell and they wanted to help me. Yeah, right. I knew perfectly well that there was nothing wrong with me. Then you left school and the nightmares stopped. I demanded they help me find my friend, and though they promised to help me find you they failed. So I left," he stepped back again, lowering the knife as he continued to reminisce.

"I learned to stimulate and control my memories selectively, piecing them together into what I needed to know. Except the map. It seems I could not remember the map, and that's when I realized that I had to find you again," he smiled, and another wave of ice rolled down my spine.

"For five years I tried to find you, not knowing where to look or what to look for. Three times I thought I had succeeded, only to be disappointed," he sneered. "It was pure luck, really, that I stumbled upon you in a bookstore one day. You were leaning over a bookshelf and as I walked by I suddenly saw the map perfectly in my mind. I discovered that when I was around you the memories were crisper, clearer," his eyes drifted away as he remembered.

"By staying near you I was able to re-create the map and begin my search," his eyes grew cold, and his gaze shifted back to me. "Only it isn't here, is it?" I shrank away from him, sliding my feet backwards across the sand.

"The false map was quite clever; it was unfortunate that you were washed overboard and rendered unavailable for further consultation," a large bubble of spit flew from his lips, landing on my cheek. I remained speechless, standing there dumbstruck and unmoving.

"I want that treasure, Duarte, and you're going to tell me where it is," the blade of the knife had made its way back to my throat, pressing hard against my unprotected flesh.

"I don't know what you're talking about," I found my voice and used it for the only thing I could think of – denial. The blade pressed harder and I swore I felt a trickle of blood run down my neck.

"No more games, Duarte," harder, and I felt the anger rise up again. I pushed forward, even as the knife cut deeper into my flesh.

"You never meant to share it with anyone, did you?" I spat out. In answer, Travis only sneered again. "It was always your plan to cut us out, wasn't it?" Travis' sneer deepened.

"It was my plan. It was my risk. It was my treasure. But in the end, I didn't have to dispatch you. You fell overboard of your own accord," he laughed and shivers ran down my spine. "A terrible tragedy, to be sure. A tragedy that deprived me of the pleasure of watching your life fade away under my hand," the knife cut deeper, and I began to wonder how much time I had left.

"You won't kill me," I finally stated matter-of-factly. Travis' eyebrows went up quizzically.

"I won't?" he asked.

"No. I'm the only person who can get you what you want, and that makes me just as valuable as your precious treasure," my heartbeat calmed.

"You're right," Travis agreed. "I won't kill you. But I can torture you so slowly that you'll wish I had killed you. And after you tell me where the treasure is, I'll be merciful and end your life quickly," the grin was back, and he shoved me hard, pushing me to the ground. In one quick motion I grabbed a fistful of sand and flung it at his face, stumbling to my feet and running back through the brush, back toward the beach where I'd landed.

As I half-ran, half-crawled along the trail I could hear Travis behind me, swearing and spitting as he clawed through the bushes. After a seeming eternity, and with no real plan in mind, I cleared the mangroves and ran out onto the beach. A loud curse from behind me caused me to turn, and I failed to see the large rock on the beach directly in my path.

I landed on my back with a thud, my head knocking the side of another, smaller rock. Travis landed on top of me and the knife once again found my neck. His breathing was short and heavy, his eyes raw and red and his hand trembling with anger, so that the blade carved small, superficial cuts into my skin.

"You're gonna wish you hadn't done that," Travis sneered, raising the blade to my face. I closed my eyes, bracing against the pain that was forthcoming. Instead of searing pain, however, I heard three distinctive rolling clicks.

"Drop the knife, Turney," a cool voice ordered. I opened my eyes and stared at the man who had stepped out from the bushes behind Travis. For a moment I was certain I had hit my head harder than I thought and my vision was distorting the images in front of me. I blinked rapidly a few times and then looked again. It was like looking into a mirror, only the mirror projected an image that was fifty years older than the original standing before it. In his raised arm he held a gun, and it was pointed directly at Travis' head. Stepping out of the bushes behind him were Thin and Eyebrows, who each held a gun of their own, both of which were also aimed at Travis. Unlike the surreal mirror image standing before me, who was dressed in dress slacks and a crisp linen shirt, Thin and Eyebrows looked oddly out of place, dressed in flowery Hawaiian shirts and tan shorts.

"You okay, CJ?" my double asked, his eyes on Travis as Travis slowly raised his body up off of mine, dropping the knife into the sand and lifting his hands into the air. A friendly smile lit his lips, and he shrugged his shoulders.

"Hey, I was just showing my friend here how to disarm an aggressor with a knife," he said casually. "He's got a bit of a thing for pirates," he leaned forward toward Thin as if sharing this news in confidence.

"Save the shit, Turney. You're coming with us," Thin indicated with his free hand and Eyebrows stepped forward, stowing his gun and producing plastic restraints from his rear pocket. He firmly held Travis' arms behind his back, cuffing him.

"Who are you?" Travis' friendly demeanor was replaced with innocent defensiveness.

"Don't worry, we'll have plenty of time to discuss that," Thin lowered his gun and smiled, patting Travis on the back. Eyebrows led Travis off, stepping into the shallow water and heading toward one of the boats anchored near mine. Thin stretched an arm down to me, but I declined, pushing myself to my knees and standing up.

"How'd you find us?" I asked as I brushed sand from my shorts and shirt. My double shook his head, and I had the distinct impression I'd just asked a dumb question.

"I was asked to look after you."

"Asked? By who?"

"That's not for me to say. Best to consider it a family thing," my double smiled. I started to shake my head in confusion and then stopped. Family. Could it be?

"Uncle Alexander?" I asked, nearly gasping the words out.

"Ah, so you *have* heard of me," he smiled.

"I thought you were…" I stopped; there was no way to proceed without sounding rude.

"Fiction?" Uncle Alexander finished, a small smile lighting on his lips. I nodded. "I'm not surprised. Truth is I'm not as bad as your mom thinks, but I know my chosen profession and lifestyle has always made her uncomfortable. I was pretty surprised to get your dad's call, but then again, a parent's instinct to protect their child overrides pretty much everything else." I nodded, speechless as I recalled all the stories I had heard about my Uncle Alexander while growing up. They seemed different now, knowing that they were likely more fact than fiction. No wonder Thin and Eyebrows seemed unlikely government agents–they were the farthest thing from that.

"Any chance you know what he was looking for?" Uncle Alexander asked, pulling me back to the present. He gestured around, "He's been tearing up land around here, looking for something," he added. He looked at me expectantly.

"Oh yeah?" I said, offering nothing and holding his gaze confidently. "I can't say that I do." I braced for the inevitable questions about what drew me out here, but they didn't come.

"Well you can be certain that he won't be able to look again, at least not for a while," Uncle Alexander turned, facing out toward the boat where Eyebrows sat with a surprisingly docile Travis.

"What's gonna happen to him?"

"Better not to tell you," Uncle Alexander said simply. I agreed silently–I didn't want to know. Thin sensed the conversation was over and started to walk out to the boat. Uncle Alexander patted me on the back, awkwardly, and turned to join them. As they approached the boats, Thin joined Travis and Eyebrows, while Uncle Alexander got into the second boat. I stood quietly, watching them raise their anchor and motor off to the east, back to Key West and civilization. Travis kept his face turned to me even as they disappeared on the horizon, and I was certain his eyes were glowing red. I shivered again, involuntarily, and then turned away, trying hard to convince myself that it was finally over. Forever. I realized that the very idea was going to take some getting used to.

Chapter 24

The skiff floated lazily in the waters of the lagoon, rolling gently on the small swells. The water was shallow and teeming with life; it was no wonder that this was a fisherman's paradise.

A year had passed since my last visit to the Keys, and Alamar was finally fading into a distant, harmless memory. I hadn't had a flashback in a year, and I didn't expect to ever have one again.

With Travis' sudden disappearance came my peace of mind. My mom still questioned me relentlessly about what had happened to Travis, what the police were doing about it and if I was really okay. I still hadn't told her, or anyone, the truth, and I was quite certain that I never would. After all, who would actually believe it?

I glanced around at the islands that surrounded me like a large, misshapen horseshoe, and let my gaze steady on the largest one to the northeast. It was known as Entrance Key, and it was completely off-limits, by order of the US Government.

I glanced down at the metal detector and small shovel lying at the bottom of the skiff and smiled.

Sometimes it's worth it to break the law.

Printed in the United States
By Bookmasters